"Now I know you're following me."

"Guilty," Garret said with a grin, "but I wanted to know how things went with your boss."

"Why?" Connie asked, turning to face him. "So you could further rub it in that I'm teetering on the brink of unemployment?"

"You're not getting fired. From what I've heard, your show's too popular to end." He shifted so he could reach out to touch her hair. To find out if it was as silky as he remembered. Unfortunately, he stumbled and pulled out the elegant knot she'd styled, leaving her in what he thought was glorious disarray.

"What'd you do that for?" she snapped. "I'm headed to the auto parts store to apply for a job there."

Not thinking, just doing anything he could to make those sassy lips stop snapping and start smiling, he grabbed her. Sure, the gentlemanly thing would've been asking her permission for what came next, but what the hell?

A gentleman wasn't something he'd ever claimed to be.

And so he kissed h

Dear Reader,

What a fun ride this book was, from the standpoint that I've always had a secret thing for navy SEALs and my hero just happens to be one! I've been waiting a long time to try my hand at this sort of thing, but was daunted by the fact that I'm about as far from being military as a girl can get! That said, I thought if I can't go to a base or aircraft carrier, why not bring my own SEAL, smoldering Garret Underwood, home to Oklahoma?

Even with a busted leg, Garret brings an extraordinary amount of chaos into his old flame's life. Uptight Constance puts up a valiant fight to resist him, but *puh-leaze*, he's a navy SEAL! Nuff said. <g>

A major shout-out goes to photographer Carl Deal, who gives an amazing glimpse into SEAL life on his Web site, www.carldeal.com/seal.html. Not just logistics and fun lingo, but deep into these men's hearts. I was deeply touched by the whole SEAL history and philosophy.

Will Constance finally give in to the temptation of her very own military man? I'm not telling! You'll have to read the book to find out.

Happy reading!

Laura Marie

Her Military Man
LAURA MARIE ALTOM

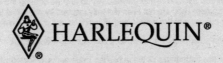

HARLEQUIN®

TORONTO • NEW YORK • LONDON
AMSTERDAM • PARIS • SYDNEY • HAMBURG
STOCKHOLM • ATHENS • TOKYO • MILAN • MADRID
PRAGUE • WARSAW • BUDAPEST • AUCKLAND

ISBN-13: 978-0-373-75151-8
ISBN-10:   0-373-75151-6

HER MILITARY MAN

ABOUT THE AUTHOR

After college (Go Hogs!), bestselling, award-winning author Laura Marie Altom did a brief stint as an interior designer before becoming a stay-at-home mom to boy/girl twins. Always an avid romance reader, she knew it was time to try her hand at writing when she found herself replotting the afternoon soaps.

When not immersed in her next story, Laura enjoys an almost glamorous lifestyle of zipping around in a convertible while trying to keep her dog from leaping out, and constantly striving to reach the bottom of the laundry basket—a feat she may never accomplish! For real fun, Laura is content to read, do needlepoint and cuddle with her kids and handsome hubby.

Laura loves hearing from readers at either P.O. Box 2074, Tulsa, OK 74101, or e-mail: BaliPalm@aol.com. Love lounging on the beach while winning fun stuff? Check out www.lauramariealtom.com!

Books by Laura Marie Altom

HARLEQUIN AMERICAN ROMANCE

1028—BABIES AND BADGES
1043—SANTA BABY
1074—TEMPORARY DAD
1086—SAVING JOE*
1099—MARRYING THE MARSHAL*
1110—HIS BABY BONUS*
1123—TO CATCH A HUSBAND*
1132—DADDY DAYCARE

*U.S. Marshals

Don't miss any of our special offers. Write to us at the following address for information on our newest releases.

Harlequin Reader Service
U.S.: 3010 Walden Ave., P.O. Box 1325, Buffalo, NY 14269
Canadian: P.O. Box 609, Fort Erie, Ont. L2A 5X3

This book is dedicated to all SEALs out there protecting our country, and to two special warrior women closer to home—Karen Lairmore and Debbie Parks. Thanks, ladies, for all the Pom rides, and most especially for the fun you've shown not only to Hannah, but to me!

Special thanks to megatalented military romance novelist and my very own navy expert, Rogenna Brewer, for filling in those last-minute, impossible-to-find details! Any errors are mine and the glory is hers!

Special thanks also to Dr. Cynthia McCoy for not carting me off to the loony bin for asking, "I have this guy, and he needs to break his leg jumping from a helicopter onto the rolling deck of a ship. Can you tell me what kind of break it would be?"

Chapter One

"Pardon my French, lady, but that's a load of—"
   Beeeeeeeep.

"My, my…" Constance Price, aka Miss Manners, said with a relieved sigh. How could it be Wednesday when it felt so much like Monday? Thank goodness she'd hit the censor button in time to avoid the juiciest portions of her caller's rant from hitting Mule Shoe, Oklahoma's airwaves. She liked to think her talk radio program was progressive, but not in a vulgar, do-any-stunt-for-ratings way. Monday through Friday, noon to 2:30, she prided herself in tastefully providing listeners with lifestyle tips on everything from hosting the perfect dinner party to sharing the perfect relationship. Sounded great in theory, but when it came to the whole guy-girl thing? Her own life hadn't turned out so hot. That said, how had she landed the job as Mule Shoe's queen of manners? Well, the show she'd originally pitched had had more of a Martha Stewart domestic-type theme. Much to her daily consternation, to expand the advertising base, Constance's boss had tagged on the show's relationship portion. Of course, that sometimes opened the door to a lot of opinionated listeners.

"Thank you, sir, for your enlightened view."

"Enlightened, my—"

Beeeeeeeep.

"Thanks again," Constance said before disconnecting the caller, then taking a hasty sip of a Diet Coke she wished had a bit more kick—with an unladylike poke of rum! "All right, as a refresher to my listeners, today's theme is breakups—how to handle them in a mutually respectable and mannerly fashion. Renee-Marie," she asked her show's redheaded Cajun producer and the station's part-time receptionist, "do we have another caller?"

"Line two," Renee-Marie said with a wink.

A wink?

Shaking her head, Constance hit the feed. "Miss Manners here. How may I assist you in living a more civilized existence?"

"Okay," the same obnoxious caller said, *"I get the hint about toning down my language. But while you've been sitting in your no doubt pink satin broadcast booth, I've been off serving our country*

in godforsaken places you couldn't imagine in your worst nightmares."

"Sorry…" Constance glared at Renee-Marie who'd held up a note that read, Felix made me do it! Felix was the station owner, her boss and a royal pain in Constance's derriere. "Truly, I am, but—"

"Look, all I'm trying to say is there's no such thing as a mannerly *breakup. I usually wouldn't have time for rehashing ancient history on a show about manners, but I've been laid up with a busted leg, giving me far too many hours for reflection. Case in point, I once knew this girl—let's call her Lucky—well…"*

Chills ran up Constance's forearms.

A million years ago back in high school, Garret used to call her Lucky—on account of her being his lucky charm. Long story short, if ever there'd been a textbook example of an unmannerly breakup, theirs was it!

"…Lucky was a looker. In fact, she reminded me a lot of you. Oh, she put on a great self-effacing act. You know, acting all demure and polite about what a closet sex kitten she truly was, but let me tell you, that girl could purr."

Constance cleared her throat, loosening the collar of her high-necked, long-skirted, prairie-style dress in the process. "Might I remind you this is a family show. Please refrain from the more base details of your story."

"*Yes,* ma'am..." Was that a mocking grin behind his words? Garret used to do the same thing—tease her about being too formal. Like she'd been born a century too late. "*So, like I was saying, Lucky—*" he coughed "*—better known as* you—*pretended to be one thing, but inside...*" His sad laugh rang over otherwise dead air. Dead. Out of necessity, the way things had been left between them. "*Anyway, without airing dirty laundry, all I'm trying to say is how about not just laying all the guilt for poorly done exits on guys? As in the case of a certain lucky charm I used to know, there are some she devils out there deserving credit.*"

Air.

Must.

Breathe.

Now.

Constance? Renee-Marie silently screamed behind the studio's soundproof window.

No way was the caller Garret.

The man hadn't stepped foot in Mule Shoe since the day he'd left for the Navy ten years earlier. Since that day, all color and hope and joy had been sucked from Constance's life. At least until her daughter—*their* daughter—Lindsay, had been born.

On the flip side, who else could it be? The guy's wrath felt targeted on her.

Really? Or was that guilt and regret over never having told Garret the truth about their little girl exploding in her head? In her heart, she'd called him a hundred times, written a hundred more letters, but somehow she'd never found the right words. How many times had she told herself fear kept her secret safely locked inside? Fear of her sad childhood playing out again? Only this time, with her daughter?

For the sake of her show—her sole means of financial support—she had to pull it together. Constance cleared her throat off air, then managed somehow to inquire in a blessedly detached voice, as if she hadn't just joined Garret's cat-and-mouse game, "Ever considered there may have been a reason behind *Lucky's* actions? That maybe she'd actually been trying to help you?"

He laughed sharply. *"By making out with another guy? Worse yet, my supposed best friend?"*

"Yes, but did you look hard enough to see if the kiss was genuine—or maybe all for show?" Covering her face with her hands, Constance told herself to shut up. The man wasn't Garret any more than her heart was on the verge of pounding straight up and out of her chest over the notion that maybe he *was* Garret, come home to haunt her. If he'd had any idea why she'd kissed Nathan that horrible night, maybe he wouldn't now be so cruel. "Maybe the whole time, this Lucky person to whom you keep referring, was kissing that other guy, she was thinking about you. Wondering if—"

"Give me a break. See? This is what I'm talking about. This show is bogus. Entirely one-sided with the favor always going to the ladies. You're always talking about how guys are basically snaggle-toothed brutes and women nothing but sweetness and light."

"That's not true. Just the other day we did a show on women who curse and how that affects the men who love them."

He laughed again, filling her mind and heart and soul with a huskier, world-weary vision of her first love. No way. It couldn't be him. No, no, no. *"I'm gone. Peace out."*

"Well…" she eventually said after a four- or five-second dead air lag to regain her composure.

Seriously, the guy couldn't have been Garret.

Last she'd heard through a friend of a friend, the Navy SEAL was rarely even in the country, let alone backwoods Oklahoma. He didn't even come home for Christmas—instead always sending his mother a plane ticket to meet him somewhere exotic.

How did she know? Strictly beauty shop gossip. Well, except for that time she'd run into his cousin

Hillary at the county fair. And then, Constance had only asked about him to be polite.

Yeah, right.

"Renee-Marie, do you have our next caller?"

"Miss Manners, my name's Pat, and I just want to tell you how much I adore your program. You don't pay that obviously ill-bred oaf the slightest bit of attention. Oh, and for the record, though I'm sixty-eight years young, and it's been fifty years since my last breakup, I still believe kindness is a virtue—most especially with those we no longer want in our daily lives."

And so the afternoon lagged on…

"Miss Manners, I'm Jim, and I gotta say I agree wholeheartedly with Military Man. All this manners stuff is hoity-toity horse crap. Oh, and just curious, how long were you two an item?"

"Miss Manners, I'm Vicki, and I agree with you in that manners are a beautiful, necessary part of life. That military man you used to date is obviously never going to land another girlfriend, much less a wife, if he persists in being such a barbarian."

"Thanks to all my callers," Constance finally said. "That wraps the show for today, so until tomorrow, I'm Miss Manners, wishing you mannerly days and deliciously refined nights."

Sharply exhaling, Constance disconnected her mic.

"Great show!" Felix burst into the drab, brown-paneled broadcast booth with all the grace and forewarning of a Sooner State twister. "Wowza, where'd you find that guy? Wait—don't answer. I don't wanna know if you two never really dated and the whole thing was rigged. But whatever you do, keep him coming. The phone's going nuts. All twenty of your faithful listeners must've called everyone they know to tell them about the show. We've had so many calls in the last five minutes, my cousin Wanda said the first time she tried getting through, there was actually a recording saying circuits are busy."

"That's all well and good," Constance said, fishing under the brown laminate counter supporting her announcer turret and mic for her worn leather purse. "But I'm pretty sure I know this guy, and trust me, he's rough around the edges. It's best we never hear from him again."

"Crap on a stick," Felix said, "you're going straightaway to sign the guy, right? Because with that much passion between you, the show's a surefire hit."

"But, Felix, I—"

He sobered. "Look, you know how I hate being the heavy, but remember that talk we had the other day?"

"A-about my ratings?" Her gaze plummeted to her scuffed brown boots.

"Yeah. How they're the lowest in this station's history—and that's saying something, considering some of the junk we've had on the air."

"But, Felix, I told you just as soon as folks realize how important caring about others' feelings and incorporating manners into their everyday lives is, that—"

"Manners schmanners," he said with a glint of his right gold canine. "All I care about are advertising dollars. Get this guy back on by the time I'm back from my trip, or your show's in the can."

Felix blustered off while Renee-Marie wandered in. They'd only been friends for a little under a year—the time Constance had been doing the show. Before that, Constance had worked more than a dozen small jobs that never seemed enough to pay the black hole of bills that came along with being a single mom.

She'd always dreamed of going to college, maybe earning a degree in history or literature to match her love of all things eighteenth and nineteenth century, back when everything seemed more…civilized. She'd fantasized about using that degree to work in a big city museum. Or the ultimate dream—penning a historic novel.

But then her and Garret's relationship had moved

to the next level, and suddenly being with him in every way a man and woman could—even though technically they'd still been teenagers—had meant more than future career aspirations. Her love for Garret had been like a living, breathing entity all its own. He'd made her feel cherished and safe and beautiful and interesting and above all, loved.

She'd have done anything for him—anything. Meaning, when she'd discovered she was pregnant a week before graduation, she'd loved him enough to let him go. To want him to follow his own dream of getting out of Mule Shoe, out from under his deceased father's lengthy shadow.

"Felix doesn't really mean it," Renee-Marie said, wrapping Constance in a warm hug. "About firing you if you don't track down that caller. You know how he is. Meaner than a crawdad with somebody dunking his tail in boilin' butter. This'll all blow over."

Constance wished she could be so sure.

One thing was for certain, if the caller was Garret, he'd be easy enough to find. His mother lived only ten miles from Constance. All she'd need do was head that way, then politely inquire whether or not her son was in town.

On the one hand, if the caller was him, and if by some miracle Constance got him to agree to make a few guest appearances, then what? Yes, her much-needed job would be safe, but what about her most closely held secret?

"You going to be all right?" Renee-Marie asked.

"Maybe," Constance said. Assuming Felix knocked off his foolish insistence on her old beau joining her show.

GARRET UNDERWOOD switched off the kitchen radio, wincing when the sudden movement stung deep within his bum left leg. Two months earlier, he'd busted it jumping from a helicopter onto a ship's deck in choppy seas. Diagnosis? Comminuted fracture of his proximal femur. Docs fixed him with a steel rod, meaning no cast but plenty of pain. Recovery time? A good three or more months, which—taking into account time already served—left a minimum of three weeks to go.

He was now up to his neck in physical therapy. Plenty of weight-bearing exercises that left him aching, but if that's what it took to get back on the job, so be it. His doc had yet to make a final decision as to whether or not he'd even still be fit to return to duty. He said he was waiting to see final X-rays to give his ultimate okay. Garret didn't need pictures to tell him he'd be fine. He had to be. For if he no longer had his work, where did that leave him?

Lord knew he couldn't spend the next fifty or so years stuck back in Mule Shoe.

He looked up to see his mother smiling. She calmly asked, "Mind telling me what that was all about?"

"What?"

She'd passed the morning in her garden, picking the first of that season's green beans, zucchinis, cukes and tomatoes. She'd started her crop early in her greenhouse, placing her well ahead of everyone else's garden game. At sixty, wearing jeans and a Rolling Stones T-shirt, Audrey Underwood looked a damn sight younger than he felt.

Tapping the portable radio she'd unhooked from the waistband of her jeans, she said, "I heard the whole thing. You do know Miss Manners is her, don't you? Your Constance? The station has a billboard of her out by the cattle auction."

"Yeah," Garret said, trying not to glare, but not quite succeeding. "I know it's her." How many other people in the county had heard him make a complete jackass of himself? "But even if you did hear me, what makes you think I was talking about her?"

"Oh," she said, setting her basket loaded with greens on the white tile counter beside the sink. The homey sight of her bountiful harvest completed the already disgustingly pleasant space. Yellow-flowered wallpaper set the tone for white cabinets and a worn brick floor. The flood of sunshine streaming through every paned window on the south wall didn't do much for his mood, either. Where was a stinkin' cloud when a guy needed one? "Maybe I don't believe you're over her because even after all this time, you still won't say her name."

Laughing, shaking his head while wobbling to his feet, he said, "Give me one good reason I should? That girl's a snake."

"That girl's a woman now."

He snorted. "A woman who ran off and married my best friend, then had his kid."

"They're divorced. Have been for quite some time."

"And I'd care why?" he asked from in front of the picture window overlooking blue sky and rolling green pasture where a half dozen Herefords stood chewing their cud. Twenty or so stubby oaks dotted the landscape that otherwise consisted of nothing much but alfalfa and ragweed reaching as far as the overgrown fencerow serving as the boundary between his mom's property and the Griggs's. Though his dad had been gone for nearly twelve years, Garret remembered like it was yesterday when the two of them used to walk that fence, checking for breaks, mostly just swapping guy stories.

Though his dad, Ben, had been an attorney by trade and only a part-time farmer, he'd loved the land. He'd made sure that financially, Garret's mother could live in the rambling two-story white Victorian plopped on the edge of five hundred acres of pasture and forest for as long as she liked or was able.

"Honey," she said, stepping up behind him, resting her hand on his shoulder. "Let it go. Let her go."

"What makes you think I haven't?"

She shot him The Look. The one he'd always hated, because no matter how many missions he'd fought, or how many hellholes he'd barely made it out of, it was a look that instantly reduced him to a scraped-knee kid all of about eight. "How do pork chops sound for dinner? Mashed potatoes. Maybe sugar peas and a peach cobbler with plenty of ice cream?"

"Don't do that," he said, swinging about to watch as she hustled back to the sink to wash vegetables.

"Do what?" she oh so innocently sang over her shoulder.

It was no family secret the woman had been after him to settle down and give her grandkids for the past five years. But if she was for one second by way of reverse psychology suggesting he look up Constance, she could forget it. He'd been trained in all manner of mental warfare and he wasn't about to succumb. "Never mind," he grumbled. "Need help?"

She winked. "Only if you're offering to get me a few dozen grandkids."

MONDAY AFTERNOON after the longest, dullest weekend ever—but wait, he'd already barely survived that the weekend before—Garret sat in an entirely too girly white wicker rocker on the front porch of his mother's house, trying to remember the last time he'd had fun.

For mid-April, the heat was fierce. Hot sun made even the usually blaring cicadas too weary to sing. Having been based on the East Coast for so long, he'd forgotten what Oklahoma heat was like—and this wasn't anywhere near the prime of it.

He swigged bottled water, wishing it was beer, but his mom had strict rules about not drinking before five, and seeing how he was already in piss-poor shape, it probably wasn't that hot of an idea to screw up his liver in addition to his leg.

Lord, how he wanted out of Mule Shoe and back to his own place in Virginia. Not that he was in the studio condo all that much, but it was the point of the matter. He needed his own space.

Far from memories being back here evoked.

Hard to believe that after all this time, after all

he'd been through, all that old angst over Constance was still there. Simmering just beneath the surface.

Sitting here in the sweltering sun, if he closed his eyes and held his breath, he'd be back to their first time.

A sun-drenched May afternoon when he'd picked her up in Big Red—his old Chevy truck—for a day at the swimming hole on the backside of the Underwood land. The pond had a rock bottom and was spring-fed, meaning the water was clear and cool. Stubby oaks and maples and a few odd cedars provided dappled shade, save for the one grassy bank his dad had cleared for his mom years earlier where he'd planned on building her a gazebo. He'd died before making it happen, but at that moment, seeing how perfect the spot was for Constance to settle her oil-slicked bikini-clad bod on top of her towel, Garret was damn glad there wasn't a gazebo mucking up the view.

Lord, Connie had been beautiful. Legs so long that every time he'd seen her in her cheerleading uniform, he'd been glad for the protection of his own football uniform's cup.

The afternoon started out casual enough as they shared chips and Twinkies and talked in the blazing sun. Not before and not since had he ever felt more comfortable opening himself up to a woman. She'd had this way of looking at him—

staring right into his soul. Made him spill secrets that in retrospect had been better off left inside. But he'd been a kid. Stupid in love. Stupid in the way she'd made him feel like the star of her life. As if being with her, he could do and be all things. With every part of his being, he'd secretly fantasized that one day, Connie would be his wife.

Later, they'd swum and laughed and took turns dunking each other. But then, he wasn't even sure how, maybe because of the way water drops sparkled in her dark hair, he'd kissed her.

They'd been going out since just before Halloween, so it wasn't as if he hadn't kissed her before. Hell, most Saturday nights they'd round second base, sometimes even third, but something about this day was different. Never had they been so absolutely alone with nothing bearing witness but the blue, blue sky and a few chattering squirrels.

Maybe he'd kissed her with such urgency because it would be a long time before he saw her again.

In his heart, where it mattered, she'd always be his. For the time being, though, he'd known parting ways was for the best.

He'd already signed his enlistment papers, seeing how for as long as he could remember, he'd wanted to join the SEALs's legendary ranks. She'd be heading off for Norman—to the University of Oklahoma, where she'd be taking godforsaken history courses that'd put him in a coma. Truthfully, other than burning lust for each other, they didn't have a thing in common. She was book smart. He was a jock, obsessed with getting in tough enough physical and mental shape to make it through BUD/S training.

With all that in mind, mixed with a good dose of apprehension and excitement for his future, too young and stupid to have put on the brakes for nobility's sake, Garret had kissed her more. Then, with a big romantic whoosh, hefted her out of the water and into his arms, carrying her back to their towels and the sun.

Hot as it was, it didn't take two seconds for them to dry and for the realization to kick in that, come mid-June when he shipped out for boot camp, it'd be a good, long while before he saw Connie again. At the thought, emotion swelled his chest, making it so tight, he hurt.

For the longest time, they just stared at each other, and then they were kissing again and he was fumbling to untie her bikini top needing her so bad he could hardly think. Every time she moaned against him, she made him want her more, so when she arched up to meet him, they were both struggling to yank off their still-damp swim bottoms.

Sweet lord, she'd been hot and slick and welcoming. The first few seconds had been awkward, but then she'd pulled him back for another kiss, and the rest was history.

A sweaty, crazy erotic joining that by all rational accounts of first times shouldn't have been that great, but to his way of thinking, was just about as close to heaven as he'd ever get on this earth.

After their first time, for those precious last few weeks before graduation, they'd discovered practice really did make perfect.

Now, see? he thought, rolling the sweating water bottle along his forehead. Memories like that were no good. He'd loved her, had hoped to marry her when he'd returned from training. To have caught her kissing his best friend stung— bad. He had no need for her, either in or out of bed.

As for Nathan, he hadn't spoken two words to the guy in the past ten years.

Garret eyed a rising dust cloud caused by a small sedan flying down the dirt road running in front of his mother's house. A faint breeze carried the dust storm right up onto the front porch, leaving him coughing and feeling none too kindly toward whoever the too-fast, inconsiderate schmuck was who'd just now turned into his mom's driveway.

Taking another swig of water, he watched through narrowed eyes as the dust settled, but sun glinting off the windshield made it impossible to see the driver. Whoever it was turned off the engine, took a second, then opened the door with a screech loud enough to startle a fence-sitting crow into cawing flight.

The driver rose, giving him a view of sleek, dark hair attached to a creamy-complexioned face partially obstructed by oversize black sunglasses. Dressed in a severely cut black pantsuit, she took her time tiptoeing—no, prancing—across the gravel drive. Didn't want to scratch those three-inch heels?

The closer the woman came, the more his stomach fisted.

No. No freakin' way.

Hidden as he'd been by sweet-smelling lilac bushes, Garret guessed he must've been as big a shock to Constance as she was to him. Only no, that couldn't be, seeing how she was invading his turf.

"Garret," she said, holding out her slim, lily-white hand for him to shake.

Trying hard to be adult about the situation, Garret nodded from where he sat, then crossed his arms. With the image of her sun-bronzed naked body still burning behind his eyes, the only thing he could think to say was a slow-drawled, "See you've been keepin' out of the sun."

Chapter Two

"Is…is that why you're in town?" Constance asked, ignoring the man's ridiculous question while withdrawing her hand. She gestured toward his left leg, which, judging by the odd angle at which he held it, he seemed to favor.

Never had she been so glad for the protective cover of sunglasses so he wouldn't see her gaping at the man he'd become. Garret had always been a big boy, but now…

Her mouth went dry, trying so very hard to forget their last few days—and nights—together.

Now…Garret Underwood was all man.

Even slouching as he was in one of his mom's feminine wicker chairs, there was no hiding the sinewy strength lurking beneath the too-tight sleeves of his camo-green T-shirt. His chest and shoulders were broad, his chiseled facial features and molasses eyes stone cold. Even his dark, spiky, short hair looked foreboding, as though any warmth he might've once had toward her was long gone and never coming back.

His only answer to her question about his leg was "Yep."

"How long have you been back?" she asked, forging ahead not because she wanted to, but because her boss had given her no choice. As a single mom, she had responsibilities that went far beyond what she *wanted* to do. In making sure Lindsay was always comfortable and happy, Constance had mastered the sometimes tough art of doing what she *had* to. Period. Yes, talking to Garret was awkward, but it had to be done. Which was why she was now sucking it up and trying to make the best of what he had apparently decided to make an untenable situation.

"Too long."

Maintaining a polite front, she said, "It was, um, lovely talking with you the other afternoon. Assuming that was you who called my show?"

"You know damned well it was me, and how 'bout we skip the small talk and get straight to business." He straightened with catlike ease that belied his apparent injury. "Why are you here?"

"Nice to see you, too," she said, glancing away from him to the far-off garden where his mother staked tomatoes. A bee hummed nearby, close enough for Constance to hear, but not give her an excuse to run.

He just stared.

"All right," she said with a sigh. "If that's how you want it. Truth is, this is the last place I want to be, but that big mouth of yours has me over a barrel."

Wishing he'd had the foresight to grab his sunglasses before heading out to the porch, Garret winced. As much as he despised the cheating wench, he still wanted her with a biting clarity he hadn't felt since…

Well, since the last time he'd seen her ten years ago.

"And…" he said, coaxing her to continue with his hands, wanting more than ever to be a million miles from this town, but most especially, this woman.

"And—" she notched her proud chin higher "—as much as it pains me to say it, I need you." Head bowed, she slipped off her jumbo glasses, allowing him a sight he doubted she wanted him to see. Her big blue eyes were red-rimmed and swollen, as if she'd spent the night crying. Why?

"The only way I can keep my job is if you agree to guest star on my show. Apparently—" she cleared her throat "—the fine folks of Mule Shoe prefer you over me."

Judging by her defeated posture, she believed what she'd just said.

What? He hadn't for a second thought her tears had been about him, had he?

"Seems to me," he said, telling himself he didn't care if her show was tanking, "what folks like isn't so much me, but conflict. Something they don't get a lot of when it comes to your show's usual fare."

"So you're an expert?" she said, bristling.

"Mom's your biggest fan. In the time I've sat around here healing, I've heard enough of your show to realize you're a more effective sleep aid than a case of NyQuil."

Scowling, shaking her head, she said, "Apparently, the years we've been apart haven't been kind. They've turned you into a jerk."

Bracing his hands on the rocker's arms, Garret sprang to his feet, too late remembering he just happened to be short one leg, leaving him wobbling. Reaching for support in the form of soft curves.

Must've been instinct that had her reaching out to help, because judging by her forked tongue, she didn't hold him in high regard. Tsk-tsking, he shook his head. "You must not be too ferocious, otherwise, you'd have let me fall."

After swiftly releasing him, then delivering one last glare, she turned, marching across the porch and down the stairs.

When she'd reached the brick sidewalk, he called, "After what you did—sleeping with my best friend, having his kid—it'll be a cold day in hell before I help you, Connie."

Her sexy derriere still to him, she froze.

"You and Nathan…"

That made her spin back around, blue eyes flashing fire. "That part of my life's ancient history."

Scratching his jaw, he chuckled.

"Notice, I'm not laughing," she said.

As if he cared.

"Garret, come on. Lose the chip on your shoulder. What happened with Nathan might as well be a million years ago. I need this job and, according to my boss, getting you in the studio is the only way I get to keep it."

Arms crossed while he leaned against a porch post, he said, "No."

"You've changed," she said, scavenging through a bedraggled black leather purse, then drawing out keys. "I used to carry a soft spot for you, asking for your safekeeping every night in my prayers, but no more. After turning down my request without even considering it, for all I care, the devil can have you."

While she stormed across the driveway, this time apparently not caring if gravel gnawed her shoes, Garret laughed. Ironic how he'd just been lamenting that he never had any fun, when the best entertainment he'd had in years had just magically appeared.

Tottering inside for that beer, taking a moment

in the living room to let his eyes adjust from bright sun to gloom, Garret had to wonder himself what'd led him to flat-out turn her down.

Truth? Lovely though Constance still was, he couldn't stand the sight of her. In his whole life, no one had ever done him so wrong. He'd loved her. Believed with everything in him she'd loved him, too. He shouldn't have even been listening to her stupid show, but with his mom blaring it every afternoon, Constance's raspy bedroom voice was hard to ignore.

Dammit, he thought, hobbling into the kitchen, yanking open the fridge. Cool air washed over him, cleansing the heat just looking at her had brought on. From the moment Constance had stepped those long, long legs up onto his mama's porch, he'd been back to exorcising demons. Rehashing what might've been.

Popping the top on a longneck Coors, relishing that first endless swig, Garret sadly came to grips with the fact that no matter how hard he'd tried, no woman had ever done it for him like her.

There. He'd admitted it.

And fire hadn't fallen from the sky.

The world wasn't about to end.

Only the very notion was nuts. In his line of work, gorgeous women came on to him every time he came up for air. But while a surprising number of his friends had snagged those women, then married them and the whole nine yards, Garret wanted no part of it. If he didn't know better, he'd say whatever happened between him and Constance had been like slow-acting relationship poison. Oh, make no mistake, he loved women in all shapes and sizes, but as far as surrendering his heart and soul to one?

After another swig of beer, he chuckled. He'd already tried that and it hadn't worked out.

"Long time no see."

From her place in the feed store's lengthy Saturday-afternoon line, Constance jumped, turning to see what oddly familiar-sounding man had crooned the words in her right ear. "You," she said, eyeing Garret.

"Not happy to meet again?" he asked. Even favoring one leg, he'd managed to sling a fifty-pound feed bag over his shoulder. He wore khaki cargo pants and another camo-green T-shirt that clung to his chest the way she used to.

She flashed him a half smile, wishing that two years earlier when Lindsay had asked for a live bunny for Easter, she'd said no. If she had, she wouldn't now be stuck in line waiting to pay for bunny chow.

"Missed me that much, have you?" His words

were spoken low enough that only she could hear over the bustling crowd of at least fifteen talkative old geezers and two crying babies. A blaring Conway Twitty song and a baying hound out in the bed of Tom Neilson's truck added to the chaos.

Shoulders straight, she said, "I have nothing to say to you."

"Funny, seeing how there's plenty I'd like to say to you." He followed her when it came time to move up in line. "Town gossip says your boss is out of town and you need me to agree to your request before he gets back. A million years ago, I'd've done damn near anything for you. Now…" He looked her up and down, his gaze so hot it left her chilled. "I'm not as charitable."

She made the mistake of glancing over her shoulder to gape, only to catch him wink. From there on out, she kept her mouth shut and carefully stared straight ahead.

Who'd told Garret Felix had left?

Oh, who was she kidding? In a town the size of Mule Shoe, Felix and his wife attending a Vegas broadcasting convention was big news.

They moved up in line again, only instead of Garret vanishing from her world and prospering elsewhere, as per Connie's wishes, he doggedly kept behind her. Did he have to smell so good? Like earth and wind and sweat and sea—which was stupid, really, seeing how smack-dab in the center of Oklahoma, there wasn't a whole lot of sea in sight!

"Hey, Miss Manners," Harvey, the store owner and checkout clerk, called when mercifully, it was Constance's turn at the register. "How's Lindsay's bunny brigade doing? She ever unload all those babies?"

"She, um, sure did—all but one she couldn't bear to part with."

"Yep," he said with a friendly chuckle. "Reminds me of my own girls. Just be grateful your little one doesn't have an affinity for horses. Now there's some real money."

"Don't I know it," Constance said, pulling out her wallet, thankful not only that her daughter preferred small livestock, but that she was almost free of Garret.

Harvey finished ringing up Lindsay's Vitakraft Rabbit Menu and Funny Bunny Fruit Bites, then said, "That'll be $14.68."

She opened her wallet, only to find herself short the $4.68. "Um…" Something would have to go back. She'd thought she still had fifteen left from buying groceries that morning, but she'd forgotten she'd had to buy toothpaste and floss, which had forced her to make a last-minute stop at the drugstore. Eyeing the bunny treats, she picked up the brightly colored bag. "Without these, how much?"

"Here," Garret said, slapping a five on the counter.

"Thank you, but no," Constance said, as if his money were contaminated, plucking it up with her thumb and forefinger, then turning to hold it out to him.

"Oh, come on," he said. "My money's just as good as anyone else's. And anyway, I'm not buying that rabbit candy for you, but your kid."

"She doesn't need your charity."

"Look," Garret said under his breath, leaning forward to talk in her ear. "Just because you and I have issues, don't punish her. I like kids. Take the money."

Harvey stood staring, then put his fingers to his lips and nodded. "I know you. You're Ben Underwood's boy. Aren't you a Navy SEAL?"

"Yessir."

"I'll be damned. Shoot, your money's no good here, son. Constance, you just run on along, and take those treats with you. I know times are tough, so you tell that little angel of yours to stop by after school Monday and she can sweep the back room to pay for this."

"Th-thank you," she said, hustling to remove not just her purchases but herself. "I'll be sure Lindsay's here."

"Sounds real good," Harvey said with a wave before turning back to Garret. "Son, it's good to have you home. And just as soon as this line clears out, how about us swapping stories? If you remember, I put time in myself back in '44 and '45. I was there when we crossed the Rhine. And did you know…"

Outside, safe in bright sun, Constance dared to breathe.

It'd been bad enough running into Garret like that, but then running out of money, and Garret offering to buy a gift for their daughter.

Their daughter…

Hands shaking so badly she could hardly open the door of her tan '92 Civic, let alone ease the keys into the ignition once she'd set her purchases on the passenger side, Constance forced air into her lungs. All those years ago she'd made her bed the second she'd allowed Garret into it.

Leaning forward, she dropped her head against the steering wheel, praying Harvey kept Garret occupied with war stories for at least fifteen to twenty minutes.

How had her life come to this?

Constantly wondering if someday Garret would tire of playing G.I. Joe, then swoop in to take the only thing in her life worth having—her precious little girl—was Constance's worst nightmare. The mere thought of Lindsay going through the same hell she had as a child in being torn between two parents was inconceivable. Not to mention a huge part of the reason that, to this day, Constance had so closely guarded her secret.

The air in the car was stiflingly hot, even with the windows down; the air-conditioning had gone out last summer. Over the winter, she'd hoped to find funds to fix it, but then the house's hot water heater had died, so who knew when she'd have cash for luxuries like cool air?

Nathan, her ex-husband but continued confidant and close friend, had on numerous occasions offered to loan her money or just outright pay for whatever she or Lindsay had needed, but with each new offer, she'd politely but firmly turned him down. He'd been a doll all those years ago to help her out of what at the time had seemed an insurmountable problem. Never did she want to burden him again.

A decade ago, the three of them—Garret, Nathan and she—had been great friends. Then she and Garret moved beyond friendship. Suddenly, pregnant, scared and refusing to bog down Garret's life by telling him of the baby, she'd confided in Nathan, hoping he'd have suggestions for what she should do. Never had she expected him to propose marriage!

Though her initial reaction had been a swift hug

and an equally speedy refusal, he'd explained that as a lifelong friend, he loved Garret, too. He wanted him to follow his dreams. Garret was too young to be burdened with a kid. When Constance had pointed out so was Nathan, he'd brought up the practical matter of his healthy trust fund. A baby and wife would be no financial burden. As for the demands on his time, he'd begged her to let him do this. Not just as a favor to her, but to Garret. Years later Nathan had admitted he loved her—had always loved her. He'd hoped she'd feel the same, but how could she when Garret had already claimed her heart?

Of course, in retrospect, Constance saw the mistake she'd made in keeping Lindsay from Garret all these years. But seeing a problem and knowing how to fix it were two different things.

Not long into her and Nathan's marriage, when Constance still slept in her own bed, dreaming of one day reuniting with Garret, Nathan had been kind enough to see her through her pregnancy. Shortly thereafter, when she'd caught glimpses of sadness and regret in Nathan's eyes, she'd released him from what he'd believed a lifelong obligation. As much as she adored Nathan as a friend, she wanted him to experience the same joy she and Garret had fleetingly found.

A thump on the car's roof made her jump.

She looked sharply up only to have the knot in her stomach tighten. Garret stood alongside her and, judging by the rich scent of grain, that thump had been him resting the feed bag on top of her car.

"Would you mind?" she barked. "That rough paper's no doubt scratching my paint."

He laughed. "Hate to be the bearer of bad news, sweetie, but judging by this scratched-all-to-hell side panel and that crunched front right fender, your ride's got a lot bigger issues than a wee scratch to the roof."

"That's not the point," she said. "You can't just go around tossing feed bags on top of women's cars."

"Would it be all right to toss other things up there?"

The question was so ludicrous, the look on his sinfully handsome mug so sincere, she couldn't stop the grin tugging the corners of her mouth. "Go away."

"I will, but first, answer me one thing."

"What?"

"Mom said you and Nathan didn't work out. He not paying child support?"

"What is it with you and outrageous questions? I thought the army taught respect?"

"Yeah, but I'm in the Navy." He winked. "So? Want me to teach Nathan a lesson on how real men are responsible for those they marry and bring into this world?"

"No," she said, ramming on the ignition. "I thought—and I quote—'it'd be a cold day in hell' before you did me any favors? Besides which, having you talk to Nathan is the last thing I need."

"True, I said that. But my chat with your ex would be for your little girl. Seems to me after what just happened in there, she needs help from someone in getting the child support that's rightfully hers. Might as well be me."

"Stay out of it," she said. "And whatever you do, stay away from Nathan."

AFTER AN AWKWARD, silent dinner with his mother, then a polite hour of TV watching, Garret now found himself back on the front porch sitting in a too-small rocker. Crickets chirped. The smell of damp earth from the freshly watered garden mingled with the sweet scent of potted petunias lining the porch.

Outside, all was calm, so why, inside, did Constance's request for help still haunt him?

Why did he care what happened with her job or Nathan?

It was a simple issue of right and wrong. Lots of times during grueling runs and missions, he'd had too much time to think, playing out scenarios, *what-if* dioramas of his life.

When his mom had told him Constance had

had a quickie wedding to Nathan—probably because she was pregnant—Garret had wondered *what if* she'd gotten pregnant with his child? Lindsay could've been his. Lord knew they'd been careless enough. What twist of fate had made Lindsay Nathan's instead of his little girl?

How would Garret's life have been different?

His dream of entering the Navy was a noble kid fantasy. But if he'd discovered Constance had been carrying his child, he'd have no doubt followed in his father's footsteps and been a lawyer. Sure, school would've been tough with a wife and kid, but he'd have managed. He still would've lived out his life fighting for the good guys.

So why had Nathan and Constance broken up?

Nathan had initially hidden his feelings for Connie well, but Garret had on more than one occasion suspected his supposed best friend of having a thing for her. Could anyone blame him? She'd been the school beauty. Their graduating class had numbered just under seventy, and though there'd been plenty of pretty girls, Constance had held most every title: Homecoming Queen, Miss Mule Shoe High, Head Cheerleader, Most Likely to Succeed. Nathan's folks owned the biggest ranch for miles around, and Nathan had every toy imaginable. Every *toy* that is, except for the hottest girl.

What had ultimately driven Nathan to betray

their friendship by making a play for Constance, Garret would never know. Just as he'd never know what she'd seen in Nathan to have run off with him. Another thing about Connie bugged Garret—why hadn't she gone to college? Sure, she'd had the baby, but lots of women had children and still went to school. It wasn't as if money would've been an issue, seeing how Nathan's folks were well-off.

Swiping his fingers through his hair, Garret stared into the night, wishing his stupid leg would heal. Wishing even more that it'd never broke. That way, he could've come home to see his mom for Christmas—or even better, as he'd mostly done since leaving, sent her a plane ticket to somewhere with a beach where they could both meet up, away from gut-wrenching memories of what might've been.

Chapter Three

"Mom?" Lindsay asked, clutching Toby, her favorite rabbit, to her chest. "What's up?"

"Nothing too exciting," Constance said, looking up from the dismal family budget with a forced smile. In dusk's gloom, she sat at the rolltop desk in the living room's southwest corner, fingering the simple gold chain she always wore. Her stepfather used to sit there paying bills, as had her grandfather. Everything had worked out fine then, and it would now, too. By sheer will, if need be.

"Then how come you look so bummed?"

"Just my allergies," Constance said, pushing back the rickety, straight-backed wood chair with its cracked black leather seat. "You know how I get this time of year."

"Yeah," Lindsay said, perching on the edge of the lumpy blue floral sofa. While scratching behind the rabbit's floppy ears, she touched her chin to the top of his soft head. "I know."

"You get your current events report finished?"

"Uh-huh. I found this cool story on a girl shark who swam from Australia to South Africa."

"Sounds cool." Constance closed the spiral notebook she used to keep track of finances—or rather, their lack thereof.

"Yeah, it is. You gonna come hear me give my speech? Miss Calloway said 'cause it's spring open house, there's gonna be cookies and stuff. And the big kids are having special speakers visit to talk about jobs. Kelly's dad owns the video store. She said he's handing out free movie coupons."

"That's nice of him."

"Oh—and before I forget, Mrs. Conklin sent you some paper on a play we're doing for the end of school program. I have to learn my lines and you have to help."

"What's the play?"

"*Red Riding in the Hood*—it's supposed to teach us not to use drugs and stuff."

"Sounds good."

To get the budget further out of her mind, Constance shoved the notebook into a desk drawer, only she must've slammed it too hard as the wobbly knob they'd tried supergluing fell off in her hand.

Lindsay burst out laughing.

"Think that's funny, do you?" Constance leaped up from the desk chair to push her daughter back on the sofa and tickle her good.

"Stop!" Lindsay shrieked, giggling and snorting and tickling Constance right back. "You're gonna make me pee!"

"Then I guess it's a good thing you—"

A knock sounded on the screen door, then an all-too-familiar male voice asked, "This a private party, or can anyone join in?"

Constance froze. Closed her eyes and struggled for breath.

"Mom?" Lindsay asked. "Everything okay? Who is that?"

"No one special," Constance said, back on her feet and tidying her hair.

Just your father.

"What're you doing here?" Constance asked, opening the screen door only wide enough to poke her head through, hopefully making it clear that Garret wasn't welcome.

"Truth?" he said with a shake of his head. "I'm not sure. Guess I felt like we need to finish our talk."

"What talk?" Constance asked, glancing over her shoulder to check where Lindsay might be lurking. To her horror, her daughter stood about three feet behind her.

"Hi," Lindsay said to their unwanted guest. "Do I know you?"

"No!" Constance said after a gasp, pushing open the door, storming out, then slamming it behind her. Only, since it was a fairly puny antique wood door, she didn't get much bang for her buck.

"You must be Lindsay," he said, leaning heavily on the nearest rickety wicker chair, glancing around Connie to wave at her daughter through the screen. "I heard about your rabbits."

"I like 'em lots," Lindsay said, pushing at the door so hard in her attempt to get out that the screen's trim dug into Constance's back.

Lips pressed, Constance crossed her arms and stared off at the neighbor's pasture. When she was a kid, all the land for as far as she could see had belonged to her parents. But over the years, tough times had forced her to sell off more and more until now all that remained was the three-acre parcel the house and barn sat on.

She'd been an only child. Her parents now lived in a Galveston, Texas, retirement home where she and Lindsay visited as often as they could. But with gas prices so steep, and her car hardly reliable, it'd been six months since they'd last made the trip.

Taking a deep breath, she told her heart to resume its normally peaceful rate. Until she worked up the courage to tell Garret the truth about Lindsay's parentage, her secret would be secure.

But just to be on the safe side, while he and Lindsay rambled on about rabbits, Connie blurted, "We're busy. Now, just isn't a good time to...*talk*."

Meeting her challenging stare head-on, he said, "I need a few simple questions answered. Promise, it won't take but a few minutes of your precious time."

"Wanna see my rabbit house?" Lindsay asked.

"No," Constance said for him. "Mr. Underwood's busy, too."

"Ouch." Apparently unfazed by her cool demeanor, he shot her a slow, sexy grin, then surveyed the front porch so different from his mother's. While they'd both grown up in the quintessential white farmhouse, his mother's had fared better. Constance's home was more brown-speckled than white, seeing how more bare wood showed than paint. Flower boxes under the windows used to hold cheery geraniums, but now all they held was cracked dirt.

Weeds choked the once-thriving flower gardens on either side of the winding fieldstone walk. On her own, always working or helping Lindsay with her studies, Constance barely had time to keep the veggie garden going; no way did she have the luxury of planting and constantly watering flowers.

"Looks like this place could use some TLC,"

Garret said. The place looked as if it hadn't seen fresh paint in the decade since Garret had left, and the approach up the dirt drive showed the roof to be in even sorrier shape. A couple of forest-green shutters had gone missing, as well.

"I guess," Constance said.

Lindsay wandered out the door. "Want to hold Toby?"

"Love to," Garret said, gently taking the creature from the girl. Favoring his still-healing leg, he held the rabbit close for inspection. Garret twitched his nose right along with the little guy.

Lindsay said, "Be careful not to touch his face. That makes him grumpy."

"Thanks for the advice. Last thing I need is a rabbit bite to go along with my bum leg."

"What's wrong with your leg? It looks fine."

"I know, but it broke. Doctors had to put a steel pin in it to hold the pieces together. Until I get the all clear from my doctor, I'm supposed to be careful."

"A steel pin?" The blue-eyed, dark-pigtailed girl grimaced, looking to her scuffed sneakers. "Yech."

"Tell me about it," he said with a laugh, surprised by how natural it seemed to be getting along with a child whose very existence had caused him countless hours' grief. How many nights had he lain awake, wondering what Connie and Nathan's baby looked like? Their little girl? The girl who, timewise, could've just as easily been his? Swallowing the knot in his throat forming over a broken past that could never be fixed, he vowed that before returning to Virginia, he would resolve his feelings for the girl's mama. He'd thought himself over Connie, but judging by the simmering emotions he'd managed to hold in check since the day he'd foolishly called into her show, he was no more over their breakup than his love for any and all ice cream.

"Is that steel gonna be in you, like, forever?"

"'Fraid so," Garret said with a slight frown before handing Lindsay her pet. He just hoped that was the end of it. His physical therapist and doctor both assured him his break was healing well, but if it didn't, the issue of his returning to active duty as he'd known it was up for debate. In the meantime, Garret worked out as best he could and mostly ate right, determined not to let a broken leg diminish his physical edge.

"Does it hurt?" she asked, "having all that metal in you?"

He laughed. "Sometimes, but—"

"Lindsay," Constance snapped, "shouldn't you get to work on your report?"

"Do I have to?" the girl whined.

"Yes," Constance said, hating to be a nag, but figuring the less time she spent with Garret the better. Having him here was dangerous on too many levels. It wasn't that she didn't think he'd make a great dad, just that she was afraid. She didn't have a clue how he felt about kids. What if he'd always wanted one, and upon discovering the truth about Lindsay, he swooped in and took her off to some foreign locale, never to be seen again?

When Lindsay tugged the screechy old screen door open, then trudged up creaky stairs to her room, Constance finally felt able to breathe.

"She's a great kid," Garret said. "You're lucky."

"Thanks," Constance said, arms crossed, wishing he would just leave.

"Look, I have to ask. You seem short on money. Is Nathan not giving you any child support?"

Glaring at him, she asked, "What is it you don't get about the fact that Lindsay and I are fine on our own? The only help we need from anyone would be you agreeing to guest star a couple times on my show."

"And I already told you no."

"Why? Because you're too busy calling in to the show for the sole purpose of thrashing me?" She laughed, only the strangled sound came out more desperate than merry. "Tell me, Garret, how you can come all the way over here with a broken leg to drill me about my financial situation when you alone hold the key to me keeping my job? Only you refuse to use it?"

"My reasons for not helping you in that regard are complicated." A muscle erratically popped on his jaw. "You wouldn't understand."

Just as she didn't understand how all those years ago she'd found the courage to let him go? Yeah, complicated she understood. Just plain mean, she didn't. And it was meanness keeping Garret from doing her show.

And it wasn't mean to have kept Lindsay from him?

Ignoring her conscience, careful to keep her voice low to guard from prying, ten-year-old ears, Constance said, "Since you apparently refuse to leave, please—" she gestured toward the relic of a porch swing "—feel free to have a seat, then explain why you can't help me out with this one, simple thing."

Rolling his eyes, he straightened, then eased backward, leaning on the porch rail. "You're being melodramatic. Your job's not really in danger. From what I gather, everyone in town loves you."

"Yeah, everyone except my boss. What's wrong with you?" she hissed. "What's happened in the past decade? Because the boy I used to know would never turn down a single mom in need."

"For one thing," he said, eyeing her with a stare

so intense she felt powerless to look anywhere but at him, "I'm a man now, sugar, and I don't take crap from anyone. And what you did to me, the way you treated me, that was crap. Now you expect me to just roll over and forget it ever happened?"

"If you feel so strongly about it, then why are you even here? Why do you care what Nathan does?"

He laughed. "It's your daughter I'm thinking about—not you. Because truthfully, don't flatter yourself by thinking I want to hash things out with you for old time's sake, it's more about—" He looked sharply away, then limped off the porch. "Hell, it's none of your business."

"Garret?"

He didn't turn back, just climbed into his mom's beige Caddie and drove away.

Why was he doing this? What could he possibly want to prove? That he was better than her? Done.

Yes, as an adult instead of a scared seventeen-year-old, she realized she'd been wrong for having hidden Lindsay from him all these years, but she'd done it for his own good. Because of what she'd done, Garret had been able to go off and accomplish every one of his dreams, while she'd stayed in Mule Shoe raising a daughter on mostly minimum wage. Like his, her life was a constant battle, only in a far different arena.

But that constant struggle had made her strong.

If Garret refused to help her, then fine. She'd darn well help herself.

If that meant giving up her beloved radio job because he refused to help, then what else could she do? Since office space at the station was limited, she did most of her preshow prep work at home, but instead of dreaming up new show ideas come Monday morning, it looked as if she'd be looking for a new job instead.

"FANCY MEETING YOU HERE," Constance's worst nightmare said bright and early Monday morning.

She looked up from Pearlman's Office Supply store's back table, the one beside the two copy machines where customers laid out their projects. At the moment, her only project was a nearly complete job application. "Are you following me?"

He snorted. "Don't flatter yourself. I'm just here picking up flyers for my school presentation. What're you doing?"

She hastily covered her application. "Work for the show."

"Top secret, huh?" The smile he shot her was so crazy handsome and brimming with white teeth, her stomach lurched. The years he'd been gone, she'd told herself no man could be as steal-your-breath gorgeous as her memories had built him up to be, but she'd been wrong. In reality, he was far better than anything she could've imagined. He wore cargo-style pants again, but this time sand-toned, with a matching T-shirt that fit his muscular chest like a second skin.

"Not secret," she said, "I just don't like discussing show material before it's fully developed."

"Sure," he said with a nod and dead-sexy wink. "Might give rogue callers like me a shot at taking your hoity-toity butt down a notch right off the bat, huh?"

Despite herself, she grinned. "I might've phrased it more eloquently, but yes, that's the general idea."

"I can respect that. Well, hey," he said, gesturing toward the checkout counter. "I've got everything I need. Catch you later."

"Constance, hon…" Evelyn Pearlman, the store owner, bustled out of the storage area with a case of individual plastic-wrapped boxes of paper clips. "I hope you haven't gotten too far on that application because I just got off the phone with my sister, Marty, and she said her grandson, Lyle, could really use the job. I hope you don't mind, you know, seeing how you've been here at least thirty minutes working so hard on filling it out."

"No," Constance said, lying through her teeth while swallowing the knot at the back of her throat. "I don't mind at all. Lyle's a good kid. I'm sure he'll make a great asset to your team."

"You're a dear for being so understanding." Evelyn crushed her in a quick hug. "And you know, now that I think about it, I heard at the Chamber of Commerce breakfast that they're hiring down at the IGA, but it sure will be a shame not getting to hear your show. I can't imagine what Felix must be thinking."

"Yes, well, you know how it goes," Constance said, forcing a brave smile, daring Garret to say a word about her blatant lie as to what she'd been doing in the store.

"Well, good luck to you, dear. Hope everything works out okay. And you," she said to Garret, "come right this way and I'll add up all your things."

While the middle-aged woman bustled on ahead, Constance was less than thrilled when Garret lagged behind while she gathered up her purse, résumé, pens and Liquid Paper. She was nothing if not always prepared.

"Why'd you tell me you were in here working on your show?" Garret asked.

"Does it matter?"

"Your boss isn't really going to fire you, is he? From what I understand, your listeners love you."

"If he weren't, do you honestly think I'd've come running to you for help? Or that I'd spend my morning filling out job applications?"

"Garret, hon!" Evelyn sang out. "Your order's all ready!"

"Look, Connie," he said under his breath, "maybe we should—"

"I've got to go," she said, not taking the chance of meeting his gaze for fear of bursting into tears. "You heard Evelyn, IGA's hiring."

GARRET KNEW he shouldn't be lurking in the canned goods aisle, waiting for Constance to bolt from the IGA breakroom where she was filling out her latest application, but for some strange reason, he couldn't help himself.

He was still furious with her and Nathan, but he wanted to get a few straight answers from her about a lot of things before never seeing her again. But that was it, right?

Surely it had nothing to do with her looking so hot in her prim and proper black interview dress? Or that uptight knot she'd made of her hair that ignited all sorts of ideas about how fun it would be taking it down, seeing it streaming over her—

"Garret?" she asked, pretty lips puckered as she rounded the corner of an end cap piled with watermelon. Hands on her hips, she said, "Now, I know you're following me."

"Guilty," he said, "but I wanted to know how it went."

"Why?" she asked, chin up, marching right past him toward the store's front. "So you could further rub it in that I'm teetering on the brink of unemployment?"

Why? Good question. He shouldn't care if she lost her old job or found a new one. He *shouldn't* care, but he did. No doubt because he wanted her head in a good place when he finally sat her down to demand an explanation for the past.

Doggedly keeping after her, though it was a hassle with his throbbing leg, he said, "You're not getting fired. Your boss is just messing with you."

"And you know this how?" She shot the words over her shoulder, sidestepping two cowboy-and-Indian-playing boys and their harried mother.

"I just know," he said, following her out of the store, wincing at the bright sun. "And if you'd for one second be logical, you'd figure it out, too. From what Mom says, your boss has an ego the size of all of downtown."

At her car, she spun to face him. "You've discussed my problems with your mother?"

"Just the job thing."

"Oh—did you also mention your refusal to help with said *job thing?*"

"Think about it," he said, shifting most of his weight to his good leg just so he could reach for her hair. Why, he didn't know, but he had to touch it. To see if it really was as silky as he'd remembered. He grabbed all right, but just as he did, she shifted, and he ended up yanking down the elegant knot, leaving her in what he thought was glorious disarray. Judging by her pinched expression and rapid-fire fumbling to put her hair back up, she wasn't as pleased with his results.

"What'd you do that for?" she snapped. "After this, I'm headed to the auto parts store to apply there."

"I'd say sorry," he said, "but I'm not."

"Because you're a mean, hateful, spiteful, crass monster of a man who—"

Not thinking, just doing anything he could to get those sassy lips to stop snapping and start smiling, he lunged again, this time using her left shoulder for support while planting his right hand behind her head. Sure, the gentlemanly thing would've been asking her permission for what came next, but what the hell?

A gentleman wasn't something he'd ever claimed to be.

And so he kissed her.

Hard, soft and every way in between.

He kissed her until her stiff body cleaved to him. Until her protesting grunts turned to soft mews. Until for just a second, he got a glimpse of the way things used to be between them and the way they must never be again. He had his career.

She had her kid. All they shared was a mutually screwed-up history and apparently, a boatload of sexual tension.

When he finally stopped kissing her—not because he'd particularly wanted to, but because the store manager came out and asked them to get a room—he wanted to say something cool and uncaring, but all that came out was "Whew…"

"Y-you shouldn't have done that," she said, holding trembling fingers to her whisker-burned lips.

She was right. He hadn't even given her the courtesy of shaving before mugging all over her. But it wasn't as if he'd planned on kissing her. It'd just happened. Just as it had back in high school when they'd fallen apart.

"Sorry," he said, even though he wasn't. Deep down, though he'd never in a million years let anyone know, he was sorry for whatever led to her running off with Nathan and, in the process, pulverizing Garret's life.

"Y-you should be sorry," she said, fumbling to get in her car now that he'd retreated. "Because of you and your—" she waved her hands as if searching for what to call what'd just happened between them "—stunt, the odds of the manager still being impressed by my interview skills are nil."

"Want me to talk to him?" he asked.

"Thanks, but no thanks." Shaking her head,

putting the key in the ignition, she said, "You may not take the threat of me losing my broadcasting job seriously, but I do. I can't for one second indulge in the luxury of letting the cards fall where they may. I have to be prepared for whatever financial disaster comes my way."

"Geez, Connie, I said I was sorry. If it helps, *maybe* I'll consider making one guest appearance."

She killed the engine. The sudden silence, save for the rattle of shopping carts and a few whiny kids, was jarring, but not so jarring as the hopeful expression lighting her face. "You mean it? You'll come do my—"

"Show?" For a split second, maybe he would've agreed, but he'd suddenly realized just how unaffected by that epic kiss she'd seemed to be. Sure, she'd gone with it, seemed to enjoy it, but what then? Had she said one stinkin' word about how much she'd missed him or how she'd been a fool for ever having chosen Nathan over him? No, which was why he now steeled his jaw, and said, "On second thought, no. And from here on out, I'll just leave you alone."

Wounded pride was a bitch, but nothing compared to the sock in his gut that'd occurred right around the time it'd dawned on him that maybe the only reason she'd gone along with his kiss was to save her show.

He limped off toward his truck.

She started her car.

With any luck, aside from his upcoming speaking engagement at Lindsay's school, Garret figured he'd never see Constance Price again.

Chapter Four

"Sweetie, this is beautiful," Constance said to Lindsay Wednesday night at her school's spring open house celebration. Staring in wonder at the ingenuity of her daughter and friends and their teacher, who'd decorated the classroom in hundreds of construction paper flowers, Constance couldn't stop grinning. The intricate creations "grew" everywhere, dangling from the ceiling, desktops, walls and patches on the floor. One whimsical bloom had even found a home on the classroom turtle's sunning rock. "I'm so proud of you guys," she said, slipping her arm around her daughter's slim shoulders.

"Garret!" Lindsay said, flashing him her most special grin.

Constance cringed.

It was no secret Garret would be the evening's main speaker, but why couldn't Lindsay have avoided him? Which was exactly what Constance had been trying to do.

Her daughter had only met the guy once. How was it she was now acting as if he was an old family friend? One possible explanation chilled Constance to her core. It wasn't possible that they'd already formed a connection, was it? Like some kind of father-daughter ESP?

"I'm so glad you came!" Lindsay said. "I'm hoping Daddy does, too, but he said on the phone that he might have to work late."

"Sorry." Though Garret spoke to Lindsay, he eyed Constance as though it was her fault Nathan couldn't make it. "For him to miss something as great as this, he must've had an emergency."

"Yeah," Lindsay said, lowering her chin to her chest. "I s'pose so."

Though Constance ached for the pain her daughter was going through at the notion of her *father* possibly missing her special night, she secretly hoped Nathan wouldn't just miss it, but keep himself safely a few states away! From time to time, they'd talked about telling Garret about Lindsay, but how? When? The longer the lie had gone on, the harder it had been to end.

Nathan just had a guilty conscience eating at him. Constance had considerably more on her emotional plate. So many fears. Losing Lindsay—

not just to a custody battle, but to her daughter's understandable anger at having been lied to so terribly Constance wasn't sure mere words could ever make it right. And then there was fear for Lindsay herself. What if Garret demanded custody, but for whatever reason, Lindsay didn't want to go? Constance had learned firsthand long ago, custody fights were ugly—especially as a child at the battle's heart.

Hands on his hips, Garret surveyed the magical garden into which the classroom had been transformed, then whistled. "I've seen a lot of places, but nothing near as impressive as this."

"We worked *really* hard for weeks and weeks to have enough flowers," Lindsay said. "Miss Calloway taught us all about how they grow and are pollinated by bees and stuff. It was pretty cool, but—" she held her hands up, palms out "—I've still got paste all over me."

"That's not paste," he said, wincing before kneeling at her eye level, "but your badge of honor." Pointing to a nasty scar on his forearm, he added, "When I got this, I was afraid it'd ruin my chances with the ladies."

"Well?" Lindsay asked with a big grin. "Did it?"

"Did it what?" he teased.

"Mess up your chance of getting a girlfriend?"

"Nah. I decided I'd rather just hang out with rabbits."

Her smile bigger than ever, Lindsay nodded. "Yeah. Me, too. Bunnies are way better than boys."

"Yeah."

"Except you're pretty cool," she said, twisting Constance's heart with the continued size of her smile.

"Thanks. I think you're cool, too. And pretty." He tweaked her nose. "Don't tell her I said so," he said in a stage whisper, making a sweeping gesture toward Constance's best coral sundress that would've looked better if she'd had time to tan— not that she would've just for him.

"But your mom's looking good, too."

Lindsay giggled.

Constance murmured a red-cheeked thanks.

Seeing Garret and Lindsay getting along so well was like some crazy mixed-up blessing and curse. Of course, she one day wanted Lindsay to know her real dad. But not now. Not like this. Not before Constance had the chance to make the meeting right in not only her mind, but in her heart.

Swallowing hard to hopefully loosen the tightening in her throat, Constance sent up a silent prayer of thanks when Lindsay's petite blond teacher finally motioned for everyone to have a seat.

"SINCE I'M SURE YOU GUYS—and gals—are ready for cookies and ice cream," Garret said, spreading raucous laughter and applause through Key Elementary's filled-to-capacity auditorium, "I'll leave you with something heavy I want you to keep in mind."

The students sobered.

As much as she hated admitting it, it didn't escape Constance that every boy present wanted to be Garret and every girl had developed an instant crush on him—including Constance, who'd long since made a fan of the night's program, telling herself her flushed cheeks had everything to do with the stuffy room and nothing with the keynote speaker. The way his commanding presence had woven a spell upon the room. The way his obviously heartfelt speech rallied children and grown-ups alike.

He'd make a great dad.

And in one youthful, rash decision, she'd taken that opportunity from him. With him safely out of state, it'd been only too easy claiming her decision had been entirely altruistic.

Now…seeing him like this, she had to wonder how much of the reason she'd kept Lindsay's paternity from Garret had had to do with Constance's own troubled past.

Clenching her hands on her lap, crushing the program, she willed her runaway pulse to slow.

Garret's being back was a temporary thing.

Lindsay's secret was safe.

No one—not even Lindsay's own biological father—could take her from Constance if he didn't even know he possessed the ammunition. Unlike Constance's own father.

Paul Halburt had gotten Constance's mother pregnant their senior year in high school. Like Garret, he'd had big plans, only once his mother got wind of her son's impending parenthood, his UCLA freshman year had been traded for a quiet wedding at Mule Shoe's First Baptist Church. Two years in—according to the way Constance had heard it—he'd told her mother he was tired of feeling trapped by a wife and squalling kid. He'd taken off for greener, more exciting pastures everyone assumed, never to be seen again.

Only around Constance's eighth birthday, he'd not only found a new wife, but religion and a fortune in the stock market. Armed with a big city lawyer, Paul had launched an ugly custody battle, which her mom, stepfather and grandparents had done their best to shield her from. Abandoning Constance the way he had, the court awarded him nothing but visitation rights—which, seeing how he'd lived in Chicago, he'd rarely and then never used.

While the rational, adult part of Constance knew she was being unbearably cruel by automatically lumping Garret into the same category as her biological father, just because Connie herself had accidentally gotten pregnant and, like her father, Garret, too, had harbored plans to conquer the world, the little girl inside her ached from having a father who hadn't wanted her. Only to have him come back, threatening to topple her world. Most especially, in retrospect, Constance ached for her mother, having to go through the trauma of fighting to keep her only child.

"All of you," Garret continued, leaning conspiratorially on the podium, "each and every one of you, possess the inner strength to be a hero. It doesn't take top secret equipment or strategic planning. Just this—" he paused to pat his chest "—heart. Want to be a hero? Try helping an elderly neighbor mow their lawn. Pick up trash in the city park. Donate canned goods to your church or a homeless shelter. And if all of that still sounds too tough, try not whining when your folks ask you to take out the trash or watch your kid brother or sister."

The pint-size audience moaned at this latest request, but in a good-natured way. As if maybe, at least for tonight, they might actually take Garret's words to heart.

"Okay," he said with a broad smile, rubbing his palms, "enough yakking—let's go get the cookies and ice cream!"

"Yaaaaay!" cried a chorus of two-hundred-plus kids.

For the next hour, Constance tried congratulating Garret on his successful speech, but seeing how she still hadn't managed to get within ten feet of the local rock star, she gave up. Instead, watching him from the sidelines, munching delicious homemade chocolate chip and oatmeal and sugar cookies along with ice cream, she'd tried—and failed—not remembering what it'd felt like basking in the man's glow.

Even in high school, he'd held this power. An innate ability to captivate.

Sometimes after a winning football game, everyone charged to the field to rally around the team, but most especially, one of the team's stars— Garret. All through middle school and their first three years of high school, she and Garret had played with casual flirtation.

It wasn't until their senior year they'd acted on feelings that, for Constance at least, had grown too strong to deny. That glorious senior year, after games, Garret sought her out, and while friends and family and townsfolk gathered around him, she stood with him. Snug against him, his arm around her shoulders. If the Mule Shoe Miners beat an especially tough team, he'd occasionally heft her up onto his broad shoulders.

After the crowd cleared and he'd showered, they'd often go to friends' parties.

But before getting to those wild gatherings, he'd always manage to find some quiet, side-of-the-road spot to show her with a thousand kisses how it wasn't just any old fan appreciation he craved, but hers.

"Mom, guess what?" Lindsay asked, a cookie in each hand, her cherubic face made even prettier by flushed cheeks and a smile that lit her precious blue eyes.

"What, sweetie?" she asked in a forced bright tone.

"Miss Calloway asked Garret on a date! And he said yes!"

"She did?"

"Yeah, Emily said she heard it's just for coffee at the bakery, but still, what if they like kiss and stuff?" Her grossed-out expression wasn't quite convincing.

"I'm sure they're just going as friends," Constance said, glancing toward Lindsay's teacher to find her adoringly gazing at Garret. A fierce, hot claiming streaked through her. Though Constance had long since relinquished her hold on the man, the last thing she wanted was a front-row seat to watch another woman win him.

Win him?

Constance rubbed her throbbing forehead.

Why, when she was furious with him for refusing her such a relatively small favor as working with her at the station, would she want him?

Why? One look at him, tossing back his head in laughter at something one of Lindsay's classmate's had said, told her everything she needed to know. That he was only a beast to her. Out of revenge over her choosing Nathan over him, he'd agreed to the date. Only what he must never know is that she'd chosen Nathan *for* him. So that Garret could live out a destiny far greater than Mule Shoe or herself.

Yes, but what about your daughter? She's more precious than any career—no matter how thrilling. Had Constance had the right to make the choice for Garret? Career over family?

"Daddy!"

Great. As if Constance wasn't already wound tight enough, Nathan, arms wide-open for Lindsay to gallop into, stood at the cafeteria's main entrance. Was there any chance of him and Garret not meeting up?

Searching for Garret's handsome mug in the crowd, she found him in front of the drinking fountain, encircled by a pack of sixth graders and a few goggle-eyed teachers and moms. In response to something one of the boys had said, he arched his head back and laughed. Was it only because of how hyperaware of him she was that Constance clearly heard that throaty rumble even though from the distance? Otherwise, his voice would've been impossible to hear.

Marching toward Nathan, hoping to guide both him and her daughter out into the hall, Constance prayed Nathan and Garret wouldn't have an impromptu reunion. Not here. With Lindsay, wide-eyed, looking on.

"Hey, stranger!" Nathan called out, slipping his arm about her waist, drawing her in for a casual kiss to her cheek. "Feels like forever since I last saw you."

Lindsay giggled. "Daddy, it's just been two weeks. Remember? You came over for meat loaf?"

"Oh, yeah." Releasing Constance, he knelt to give Lindsay a noogie. "How could I forget? That stuff gave me heartburn for three weeks."

Constance gave him a playful swat. Nathan was always goofing around with Lindsay, making her feel special and wanted. How many times had Constance wished she felt half what she had for Garret with him? Nathan was a wonderful man; he deserved an equally wonderful woman to call his own.

"All kidding aside," she said in a tone hopefully only he could hear, "how about taking this out in the hall?"

"Huh?"

Nudging her head back, she whispered, "Remember how I told you Garret's back in town?"

"Yeah."

"Mom?" Lindsay asked, "Can I go see Emily?"

"Sure," Constance said, thrilled her nosy daughter would be anywhere but listening in.

Back to the matter at hand, Nathan asked, "So what's going on with Garret?"

"He's here."

"Seriously? Where?" Instead of avoiding Garret as she'd hoped, Nathan craned his neck, easily zeroing in on the one target she'd wanted him to steer clear of.

"Don't look!" she hissed. "What's wrong with you? Do you want him to see you?"

"As a matter of fact," he said, jaw hardened, "yes. That's exactly what I'd like." Grabbing her hand, giving her a squeeze, he said, "Maybe this is a sign, Connie. You know, that it's time you— *we*—finally come clean with our old friend. We've talked about this, how what we did was brash and stupid and wrong. Granted we were kids, but I see this as a chance to make it right."

Feeling hot, sick, dizzy, Constance moaned. "You want to do all that *here? Now?*"

"No. Hell, no. But would it be so bad to start a dialogue?"

Yes! It wouldn't be just bad, but awful.

Knowing her luck, her every worst fear about losing Lindsay could and would come true.

"Connie?" Aside from Garret, Nathan was the only other man to have ever called her by the shortened version of her name. How come when he said it, she felt kinship, and when Garret said it, she felt hot and bothered?

"What?" she snapped.

"Are you thinking about it? Maybe this weekend, Lindsay should stay at a friend's, then we can finally get this off of our chests."

"Yes. I'm thinking." Sort of. But at the moment, the majority of her attention was focused on Garret, resplendent in naval dress whites, marching toward them with barely a hint of a limp. Good lord, was the man gorgeous. Judging by his thunderous expression, he was also dangerous. "Thinking you might want to leave."

"I'm not afraid of him," Nathan said, straightening, extending his hand when his old friend—her old lover—approached. "Garret. Long time no see."

Garret didn't shake his "pal's" hand. Too much history simmered between them.

Hypocritical fury laced through him in knowing that as upset as he was over Nathan not helping his family out financially, Garret himself was just as cruel in withholding help from Connie. On the surface, it'd be so easy to join her at the station, but what then? How did he begin handling the inevitable emotional riptide of the two of them being together? Working side by side in close quarters? Wanting answers to decade-old questions he feared would be forever swimming in his head? Yes, he wanted those questions answered, but in one swift mission. Being cooped up with her in a stuffy broadcast booth day after day would be hell.

Connie cleared her throat. "Well…Nathan, are you ready to go?"

"No," Nathan said. "Garret, man, look, I'll be the first to admit I did you wrong, but—"

"Did me wrong?" Garret's laugh was menacing. Did the guy honestly have no idea of the wreckage he'd made of Garret's heart? God, the guys in his unit would laugh him off the planet if they knew how messed up he still was over all of this. Why couldn't he forget and forgive? Or, at the very least, be blessedly numb? "If we weren't sharing the room with a couple hundred kids, I'd deck you."

"And I wouldn't blame you," Nathan said, "but—"

"Save it." To an openmouthed Connie, he added, "Please make my goodbyes to Lindsay." *I've got to get out of here.*

"HAVE FUN?" GARRET'S MOM asked from her recliner once he got home. Folded newspaper and a pen in hand, she was doing the crossword while watching her shows. She'd spent the afternoon baking her legendary jumbo chocolate chip cookies for the elementary school, and the house still smelled of them, making his stomach growl. She'd caught a ride home after his speech with one of her PTA friends.

Did he have fun? It took every ounce of composure he had left not to burst into hysterical laughter. He'd led full-scale invasions easier than standing beside Nathan and Constance had been. A million times he'd seen them together in his mind, but actually being with them, witnessing how cozy they were despite their divorce, had left a bitter taste on Garret's tongue. "Sure. The kids were great."

"Oh?"

Bum leg throbbing—no doubt due to having put all his weight on it to appear imposing—he limped through the entry hall and across the living room to fall into the recliner alongside his mom's.

"Marge Calloway called."

"Relation to Lisa?"

"Mother. She says you asked Lisa on a date."

"Point of fact—she asked me."

"Hmm…" She focused on her next crossword clue.

"Don't believe me?"

She shrugged. "I'll just be glad to see you getting out."

His only answer was a grunt.

"Did you see Lindsay Price?"

"Constance and Nathan's girl?"

"Don't play coy. You know full well who I mean—especially seeing how Dora Meyers saw my car parked at Constance's house Saturday night—and I know I wasn't there."

"Damn, but this town has an efficient rumor mill."

"She has beautiful eyes," his mother said, filling in the answer to another crossword clue.

"Dora Meyers?"

"Oh, Garret, for heaven's sake." Smacking the paper to her lap, she said, "Lindsay. Constance's girl, Lindsay. Her eyes are lovely. Just like her mother's."

Rubbing his temples, blocking the image of Constance's gorgeous eyes—eyes he'd once trusted more than any other pair on the planet—Garret's answer was another grunt.

"Men," she said, nose back in her puzzle.

"Women," he said, pushing himself out of the chair, planning to hit the sack, but fearing sleep would be a long time coming. "Got any ice cream? And more cookies?"

"A few dozen. They're for the church nursery, but I guess you can have a couple."

"The longer I'm here, the more I'm noticing you hang out just as much at that school as you do at church. What's going on over there that's so interesting?"

Frowning, she said, "You don't find our nation's future enthralling?"

Sensing this was a no-win debate it'd be best to steer clear of, Garret retreated to the kitchen to make a few calls to friends back on base, but mostly, to be safe to fight another day.

"DON'T MEAN TO BE RUDE," Constance's latest caller said during, mercifully, the last hour of Friday's show, *"but this whole thing was a lot more fun back when your old boyfriend, Military Man, called in."*

"Thank you, sir, for your view," she said politely into the mic, the whole time clenching her fists, furious with Garret for landing her in this position. Even more upset with herself for ever making him an enemy. More still for apparently not having the skills needed to lead a successful solo show. According to office gossip, word about Garret's initial call had spread like wildfire. After that, even though he hadn't called since, her listener base had doubled. Maybe even tripled. Having a larger audience was great, but not if they jumped ship as soon as they'd hopped aboard. "Okay, to all of our listeners out there, might I remind you that today's topic is Napkin Folding—Yay or Nay. Now, in addition to discussing certain folds, I'd also like to hear your thoughts on how extravagant table decor makes you feel. Think about it—have you ever sat down at an opulently dressed table only to feel like the most underdressed belle at the ball? Come on, ladies—and gentlemen—drag out those dating disaster archives and let us know if an intimidating Swan Fold was responsible for your relationship *folding.* Renee-Marie? Do you have our next caller on the line?"

"Sure do. Yvette from Hawthorne has a comment."

"Welcome, Yvette, to the show."

"Thank you, Miss Manners," the youngish-sounding woman said with a giggle.

"You're so very welcome. Please, go ahead with your comment. Have you ever come across the Swan Fold on a date?"

After another giggle, the woman said, *"I don't know much about napkins. I mean, they're nice and all, but a little fancy for around here, and I've never had a date go bad because of them. Anyway, what I was calling about is your Military Man. A friend of mine who graduated from Mule Shoe High the year after you two said he's that hunky Navy SEAL—Garret Underwood—who spoke at*

Key Elementary's open house last night. That true?"

"I, um," Constance paused for an off-air clearing of her suddenly clogged throat. "I'm sorry, but I'm not able to disclose his identity."

"Because you don't want to?" the caller asked. *"Are you keeping him all to yourself?"*

"I, um…" Wild-eyed, Constance looked to Renee-Marie, waving her arms in the universal sign of drowning, hoping her producer would know what to do.

"Oops," Renee-Marie blessedly said, "but we lost that call. Probably a cell."

"Undoubtedly," Constance said, mouthing *thank you* through the soundproof glass.

Renee-Marie flashed her a thumbs-up.

Ten minutes faded to twenty, then thirty. Finally it was time for her trademark closing. "That wraps our show for today. So until Monday, I'm Miss Manners, wishing you mannerly days and deliciously refined nights."

Constance started Big Hal's Tires's newest ad, then sagged in her chair. Time hadn't passed this slowly since high school algebra.

Felix burst through her office door. Judging by his pinched expression, his visit wasn't social. "What was that? Napkin folding and how that louses up dates? All I can say is that you'd better thank your lucky stars for a record number of callers. No doubt there were just as many listeners hoping to catch Military Man that they inadvertently saved your behind."

"Really, Felix," she said, leaning under the counter to fetch her purse, "I promise Monday's show will be more to your liking."

"Oh, that you can guarantee. Either Military Man marches with you through the broadcast booth door, or today was your last show."

GARRET SWITCHED OFF the kitchen radio.

Thank God his mom was at some church thing. He didn't feel like putting up with either her questions or worried stares. Mule Shoe wasn't exactly a metropolis, meaning secrets didn't stay that way long.

It'd shocked the hell out of him, hearing his name on air like that. Not only had it shocked him, but made this whole mess with Constance more real and, whether intentionally or not, made him responsible for what was happening to her show. Granted, it hadn't been all that thrilling before he'd stepped in, but stepping in at all wasn't cool. If he'd just kept his mouth shut instead of going off on her like that, aside from their brief encounters at Lindsay's school or around town, her job might never have been affected.

Which, the way he saw it, left him only a couple options. One—he could pack up and leave Dodge. He'd continue his PT on base. In his last call, his pal Marchetti had suggested the same in case he was bored. Ha! At the moment, boredom was the last of his troubles. Option Two—finish his PT here, and in the meantime, step up and do the right thing by helping Connie out of this bind he'd put her in.

That didn't mean he'd forgotten the delicate matter still between them, just that he was man enough to admit when he'd been wrong.

He snorted.

Unlike Nathan.

Jaw hardened with determination, Garret stormed harder than he should've to his room, where he changed from cargo shorts and a white T-shirt to khakis and a light green golf shirt given to him by a woman he used to date who'd said it'd looked good with his eyes. Strange how he couldn't for the life of him recall her name, but he remembered the compliment because it reminded him how years earlier, Connie had said the same about some concert T-shirt he'd long since tossed.

So why was he now pulling the golf shirt from his closet? Who was he out to impress? He wasn't about to volunteer for radio duty specifically for Connie, but rather to soothe his own conscience. Whether she'd been his ex-girl or a stranger off the street, helping her was the right thing to do. What he wore had no bearing on the special op.

Sure about that, stud?

That parking lot kiss still fogging his brain at the moment, Garret wasn't too sure about anything other than before heading back to Virginia, he wanted Connie out of his life. Especially out of his head. Granted, at the moment he wasn't clear on how to accomplish that goal, but any day now he'd surely figure it out.

Chapter Five

Constance left the studio feeling lower than a rattlesnake's belly.

Heat shimmered on the station's blacktop lot, rolling in iridescent waves. The building next door was having the roof retarred, so what little air stirred was hardly fit to breathe. Worsening matters was tooth-jarring jackhammering from the road crew outside the station's front door.

Zigzagging through the alley lot that was shared with a half-dozen other businesses, she reasoned that, looking on the bright side, who needed air or teeth? At the rate her personal and professional lives were plummeting, if she didn't need to provide for Lindsay's care, Constance would've long since collapsed on some shrink's couch.

Pausing at the trunk of her Civic to fish keys from her purse, she snagged them on a surprise piece of gum that'd been hiding on the bottom, when the roar of a car speeding up behind her made her jump.

She spun around, only to put her hand to her chest. "Garret?"

"Great. I caught you." He sat behind the wheel of his mother's Caddie, looking far too handsome for his own good. "Just in time, from the looks of it." His weak smile left her unsure as to his mood. Pensive? Mildly happy? Who knew. She used to know the meanings behind his facial expressions better than her own. Now…he was stranger.

"In time for what?" she asked with an enigmatic smile of her own.

"Hop in. This may take a while and it's too hot to hang out here."

"I don't know…." She eyed him, the car's confined space. Granted, a Caddie beat the heck out of her car for legroom, but still. With their kiss all too fresh in her memory, sharing a front seat with the guy hardly seemed prudent.

Worse yet, what could he possibly want to discuss that would take *a while?*

"Come on," he urged. "Climb in. You're wasting gas."

"I have to be home by four to meet Lindsay's school bus."

"And right now," he said with a glance at a black,

high-tech watch, "it's 2:45. Promise, I'll have you back to your ride in plenty of time to beat her home."

"It's not just that," she said, shifting her weight from one leg to the other. "I just don't think it's a good idea that we talk. You know…" Flailing her free hand at her waist, she gazed at the sky rather than his direct stare.

"You owe me this much, Connie. Please."

He was right.

Nodding, swallowing a wall of fear, she straightened her shoulders, then somehow made it on quaking knees to the passenger side of the car.

The AC blasted deliciously cool air at her flushed cheeks and throat. Sitting this close to the man who had once been her world, she felt scandalously underdressed in her sleeveless, scoop-necked ivory sundress. As if despite the heat, she'd be better off in a turtleneck and parka. Wearing so little didn't just leave her body exposed, but so much more.

She wiped damp palms against her thighs.

"Nervous?" he asked, putting the car in gear, then gliding across the lot.

"A little. Where are we going?"

"Mindy's."

"The drive-in?" How many times had they been there back in high school, fishing change from the backseat of her car or his truck's ashtray for a burger and malt?

"Yeah. If that's okay?"

"Sure." He was asking her permission? After the icy meeting between him and Nathan, Constance could hardly believe Garret was speaking to her, let alone seeking her approval.

"I can't even count how many years it's been since I've had a chocolate malt."

"Me, too." Fastening her seat belt, careful to sit straight in the sumptuous leather seat, she tried focusing on anything but him. Anything but his strong hands gripping the wheel. The way those hands used to hold her…love her. Whew.

At the restaurant, a carhop took their order of two malts, then skated back inside.

Her companion cleared his throat, filling her with dread. Oh no, here it came. Whatever it was. "First, I have to admit to listening in on your show today. It was a train wreck."

"Thanks," she said without a trace of a smile.

"I didn't mean it was technically bad, but in other ways."

"Which no doubt made your day?" Removing her seat belt, the metallic click deafening in the otherwise quiet car, she angled away from him to face the window.

"Hey… Sorry. That didn't come out the way I meant. And for the record. No. I didn't feel remotely good about your show tanking. More in the realm of me having been an ass."

His admission rocked her.

"Not that I'm in any way prepared to forget what went down between us, but my life's work has been about rescuing people in need, and you, Constance Price, are in definite need of saving."

True.

As much as she hated that he had recognized the fact, she hated worse being in the position. She was a strong, capable woman. She didn't want to need Garret's help.

"That said, for as long as I'm in town, I'll help with the show."

Stunned, she sat there stone silent, squelching the crazy urge to leap across the seat and crush him in a hug.

"Well? Doesn't this merit at least a thank-you?"

"Of course," she said, eyes focused on her hands, tightly clasped on her lap. "Words can't describe how grateful I'd be for your help...."

"But..." He motioned her on.

"I guess I just—" Sharply exhaling, she blurted, "How is this supposed to work? I mean, logistically. Obviously, you can't stand the sight of me. Not that I blame you, but—"

"Stop."

"What?"

"Blabbering. Connie…" He sighed. Thumped the wheel with his palm. "Look, it's true that there are about a million reasons why I'd rather be anywhere than crammed into a broadcast booth with you every day from noon till two-thirty. But the fact is you need my help and that's what I do. Help. Be it a kid, woman or country."

"But Nathan, what—"

"Nathan's a big boy, he can take care of himself. I'm not sure when, but rest assured, he and I will have words."

"But, Garret, he—"

"Stow it. When it comes to him—" He slashed his fingers through his hair. "Time to revert back to that old 'if you don't have anything nice to say, keep quiet' rule."

"He's a good man, Garret. Really. He offers me— Lindsay—money all the time. I turn him down."

Angling on the seat to face her, he asked, "Why? Why do such an asinine thing when you obviously could use more than a few bucks?"

"I don't know," she said with a fierce shake of her head. "Pride, I guess." It was hardly fair to make Nathan pay for a child he'd had no part of bringing into the world.

"But Nathan's Lindsay's father. Your ex. There's nothing wrong in accepting what's rightfully yours. And especially Lindsay's. Talk to him, Connie."

"I have. Just like I told you, I've told him. I don't want his, or anyone else's, money. Lindsay and I have made it just fine on our own all these years and—"

Constance jumped when the carhop knocked on the window. Garret had left the car running with the windows up to preserve the blessed AC.

While Garret fished money from his wallet to pay for the drinks, Constance tried to stop her spinning thoughts. Though she didn't deserve his help, Garret had come to her, open-armed, ready to serve. He was a hero in every sense of the word, offering to come charging to her rescue, making her the worst kind of scum. Nathan was right. Had been right. Garret deserved to know the truth. And she'd tell him. Someday. Soon. Just not now. Later. Once she'd found the nerve.

"Wow," he said after paying the teen, sipping his malt while passing Constance hers. "These are even better than I remembered. If I still lived here, I'd have to have one every day."

The horror! If he still lived in Mule Shoe, she'd have to be fitted for a straitjacket!

Or, you could tell him everything, then let the chips fall where they may... She scowled.

"You all right?" he asked. "You haven't taken a sip."

She did. Faked euphoric frozen-dairy joy. "Yum."

He rolled his eyes. "It might've been ten years since I've last seen you, but I remember that tone. Spill it."

"What?"

"Whatever's obviously on your mind. I would think you'd be grateful I've agreed to do the show, but truthfully, you look terrified. You're not afraid I'll make a mess of it, are you?"

"No," she said, slurping hard enough to bring on a paralyzing brain freeze. "I have total faith in you. And in case I didn't express it enough earlier, thank you. A million times over, thank you."

Throwing caution to the wind, she set her malt in the center console's drink holder, then hugged him.

"You're welcome," he said, awkwardly patting her back while she clung to him. He felt so good. Strong. Like he could take on the world. Why hadn't she told him the truth when she'd first found out she was pregnant? Maybe he wouldn't have had to give up his dream. She'd then have a real husband. Lindsay, a real dad. They could have been a happy family. At least they could've been if she hadn't thrown it all away.

Easing back, he added, "I'm helping you, but that doesn't mean you're off the hook. One night— soon—we've got to talk. *Really* talk." He looked down, breaking her heart by the crack in his voice.

"This isn't easy to admit, but seeing you again brought all the pain back. For years, I've buried myself in work, telling myself what you and Nathan did didn't matter. I was over it. But…"

His wounded, naked expression hurt way worse than any of her own pain. She'd done this. And for what? At the time, back when she'd been seventeen and thought she'd known more than anyone in the world, she'd believed in her decision. She'd believed keeping her pregnancy secret wasn't just right for Garret but herself and her unborn child. She'd felt as if she'd done him a huge favor. Now…she felt empty. "I—I'm sorry," she said, her voice a raspy whisper. "I never meant to hurt you."

"Then why?" Angling to face her, he reached for her hands. "Why, Connie, did you marry Nathan? I wasn't going to get into this now, but it's burning me up inside. I just have to hear it from your lips. You know, the same lips that kissed him, made love to him. My supposed best friend." He snorted. "I have to know what you found in him that was lacking in me."

Nodding, silently crying, she wanted so badly to cleanse herself with truth. She wanted to, so what was stopping her?

"Tell me," he pressed, not backing down.

"Nothing. It was just one stupid night, okay?"

"When?" Garret demanded, never having felt so

out of his mind with frustration. He'd thought simply offering to help her would in turn help him deal with his feelings, but he'd been wrong. On so many levels. Most of all, that he'd never gotten over her. He still wanted her, even though he also despised her. "I need details, Connie. How long had you two been going out behind my back? Were you sleeping with him at the same time as me? If so, how do you know Lindsay's even his?"

Wide-eyed, shaking her head, she said, "I know she's his because I know."

"Not good enough." He tapped her temple. "For my own sanity, I need to know exactly what was going through your head." Holding her chin, running his thumb roughly over her lips, he said, "I have to know the precise moment you stopped loving me and started loving him."

"Why?" she cried. "It's in the past. Why can't we leave it there?"

"Why?" He laughed. "Hell if I know. Trouble is, ever since landing back in this one-horse town, ever since listening to that smoke-sexy voice of yours day after friggin' day, I'm consumed with you. God, listen to me. I sound like some crazed stalker."

"No," she said. "You sound normal. Like a man who's been betrayed."

"Well?" he prompted. "Seeing how you did the betraying, couldn't you now at least give me what I want? A few simple answers?"

"You don't know what you're asking," she said, refusing to meet his gaze. "It wasn't like you think."

"Then correct me. Tell me how it was. Was it the money luring you to him?"

"No."

"Then what?"

Sighing, tears sliding into her mouth, she sniffled. "I never, *ever,* loved him like I love you."

"Love? As in present tense?"

"That came out wrong. You know what I mean. Since you won't let it go, I think, I don't know… Maybe I turned to him—we turned to each other— out of missing you."

"Before I'd even gone? Thanks."

"You asked. I'm sorry. You'll never know how sorry, I—" Hands on his good thigh, her earnest touch took him to a new low. "You have to believe me. What I—we—did, was never meant to hurt you. It just…happened." Meeting her red-rimmed stare, for a second, he almost believed her. Almost. But how could he when the truth was in his face? Those eyes of hers were also Lindsay's eyes. She and Nathan had made a child together. Women knew who the fathers of their babies were. Garret knew that suggesting he was Lindsay's father was grasping at straws. For what? To hold on to something that was apparently never his?

"I should get you back to the station. I've already kept you longer than I'd planned."

"It's okay," she said. "It's good we cleared the air."

Did we? "Yeah."

Chapter Six

"Felix…" Connie said midway through her Monday afternoon show to the pudgy, bald guy barging into the cramped broadcast booth. While hourly local and national news was being delivered from another booth, Garret and Connie were supposed to be indulging in a much-needed breather, not entertaining. "…meet the Military Man—Garret Underwood."

"It's a pleasure," the guy said with a broad grin. Garret hadn't met him earlier because he'd been out for a long lunch. Felix's gold canine had jerk written all over it. No wonder Connie had been freaked over losing her job. A guy like him wouldn't recognize a gem like Connie if she jumped up and bit him on the— "With you on board, I smell state-wide, maybe national, syndication."

Crushing the guy's outstretched hand, meeting his brash grin with a tight smile, Garret said, "To reiterate our earlier discussion, I'm only here as a temporary favor. Soon as I get the okay from my doc, I'll be out of here."

"Oh, sure," he said, gesturing to Garret's leg. "Then we'll work something out. Have you call in. With today's technology, you could be in Thailand for all I care—just as long as the chemistry between you two keeps sizzling." He licked his finger, holding it to the wall with an obnoxious hiss. "Hot stuff."

After a few more minutes of small talk, the man finally left. Garret hoped his departure was more because he'd given Felix his most lethal stare than merely because the break had almost ended.

"Sorry," Connie said. "Under Webster's definition of *obnoxious,* there's a picture of my boss."

Sipping bottled water, Garret chuckled. "I'm the sorry one. I should've trusted you to have told the truth about your predicament."

"Why?" she asked softly, not meeting his gaze.

"Why should I trust you?"

"After the way things were left between us, I wouldn't blame you for thinking me an opportunist."

"Yes, I'm not happy you chose Nathan over me, but it happened. Sure, you could've chosen a kinder way of letting me know than me stumbling upon you, finding you kissing him in front of our friends, but I'm dealing with it." *At least in public.*

"Me, too," she murmured, running her fingers along the brown laminate counter holding the old-fashioned mics.

"Cool. Then let's leave the past in the past." *That way, when it's time for me to head back to Virginia, I won't remember this moment.* The way Connie wore her hair down and each time she crossed or uncrossed her legs in the close space, he smelled her tropical perfume and a hint of the syrup he imagined her having eaten for breakfast.

"Constance," the show's producer said over a static-filled intercom. "You're on in thirty."

Connie pressed a button, then said, "Thanks."

Garret had just taken another chug of water, thrilled to get his mind on anything but the sexy swell of Connie's bare calves when the producer said, "In, three, two…" She mouthed the *one,* gesturing for Connie to jump in.

"Welcome back," Connie said, her voice a shade husky, her mannerisms natural and at ease—despite the tic he'd noticed alongside her left eye. So…he made her nervous?

The feeling was mutual.

"Thanks for staying with us through the break. As a refresher to those of you just joining in, today's scintillating topic is Thank You Notes—Not Just For Great-Aunt Mary. I want to hear not just your tips on how to write great, heartfelt notes, but your feelings on the matter. Are you upset when you send a toaster for Cousin Tammy's wedding and never hear from her again? Are you Cousin Tammy and haven't had time to send formal thanks? Let's hear from both sides. Now, as a special treat for the next few weeks, we have an in-studio guest, Mr. Garret Underwood. An old friend some of you regulars may already know as Military Man. Welcome, Garret."

"Thanks." He tried not to snicker at again having to hash over what he considered a ridiculous subject.

"For those just joining us, would you please restate your views."

He cleared his throat. "In my line of work, we have strict protocol about this sort of thing. If the Flag's wife—sorry, Admiral in Charge's wife—so much as bakes you a cupcake, there'd better damn well be a dozen roses along with a sincere note of gratitude on her doorstep by 09:00 the next morning. The damned nuisance notes are a necessary evil—one that, if you're lucky, can be pawned off on someone you outrank. I'm all about gratitude, but personally, if I do a kindness for someone, a verbal thanks is all I need."

"So," Connie asked, "if you gave a friend's son or daughter a graduation gift, you wouldn't be offended by never knowing if they received it?"

"Not no, but hell no."

"Language."

"Sorry."

"So am I," she said with a cute scowl he had the craziest urge to kiss right off her grumpy face. "Sorry that you'd be so cavalier about a decaying part of our society."

"Huh?"

"First, our youth are slack about thank-you notes, then school, then—"

"Whoa," he said over her. "What does a waste-of-time piece of paper have to do with slacking? If a person says thank you, why isn't that enough?"

"So then phoning in a thank-you would also be sufficient?"

"Heck, yeah."

Viewing him with a pinched expression of what he could only assume was utter disgust, she sighed, then turned to the producer. "Renee-Marie, do you have our next caller?"

"Yes, ma'am. Craig's on line two."

After shooting Garret one last dirty look, his cohost switched on the charm. "Welcome, Craig. Are you a proponent of the lost art of formal thank-you letters?"

Best as Garret could tell, what he just heard was a genuine guffaw.

"Lady," the caller said, *"I run a steel fabrication shop. Let's just say that around Christmas*

bonus time, I'd take a heartfelt handshake over some sterile piece of paper with a stamp on it any—" beeeeep *"—day. I mean, my guys work hard. They should play hard, too—not spend their off time penning some stupid note that's just going to end up filed in my office trash."*

"Thanks, Craig," Garret said, "for proving my point."

"My pleasure," said the caller.

"What?" Garret asked his gaping cohost. "I take it you disagree?"

"For once," she said with a firm shake of her head, "I must've been so shocked I found myself at an actual loss for words."

"Hear that, folks?" he teased. "It's a miracle!"

"You're a beast," his fiery cohost all but spat. "Renee-Marie, next caller, please."

"Parrish on line three."

"Welcome," Connie said, fingers to her temples. Were his views giving her a headache? Good, because his proximity to her was sure causing a myriad of aches in him. "Would you be so kind as to share your views?"

"Ask me, I think that holier-than-thou, high-on-his-horse, lazy man of yours needs a swift kick in the britches."

"Let's get one thing straight," Connie said, challenging Garret with a stare, "he's not *my* man."

Garret couldn't help but chuckle. "Well, now there's a dare if I ever heard one."

"L-let's try to stay on topic," Connie said, gulping her sweating bottled water.

"So sorry for the mistaken identity," the caller said. *"The way you two carry on, reminds me of an old married couple."*

"Apology accepted," Garret's cohost said.

He, on the other hand, wasn't nearly done gnawing this highly entertaining bone. Lord knows she'd bugged the hell out of him for years. It was high time she felt a fraction of his brand of discomfort.

"Wait a minute," he said, leisurely chewing on the cinnamon toothpick he'd used after lunch. "Tsk, tsk. Miss Manners, are you telling me and all these fine listeners out there that you're not the least bit attracted to me?"

"I'm telling you to knock it off and get back on topic."

"Ouch." Hand to his chest, he said, "I'm wounded. No woman has ever minded kissing me before. You saying you'd be the first actually to object?"

"I don't know. Are you asking me for a kiss?"

"Though your Military Man annoys me to no end," the caller said, *"I'd probably break down and kiss him. You know—strictly as a tame-the-beast kind of thing."*

"Mmm, Parrish…" Garret teased, "you're seriously turning me on."

"That's it," Connie said, storming to her feet and taking her mic along for the ride. "This was supposed to be a thoughtful program on reprising a dying art—not raising your libido. Thank you, Parrish. Renee-Marie, next caller, please."

"Kelly, line six."

"Welcome, Kelly," Garret said. "You like getting thank-you notes?"

She giggled. *"Thank-you* kisses *are more fun. Go for it, Miss Manners. Kiss him. You might like it."*

Off air, Connie hissed, "Hush! You're ruining my sweet show."

"Lest you forgot," he said with a slow grin, "your *sweet* show was about to be canned without my help."

The producer chimed in with, "Welcome, Doris, you're on the air with Miss Manners and the Military Man."

"Kiss him," said Doris.

"Go on, Military Man," said Doug a short while later. *"Show her what it's like being with a real man."*

"You might like kissing him," Claire from Conway said next.

Tina in Tulsa chimed in with, *"If you don't kiss him, I sure will."*

Still grinning about having gotten under

Connie's skin, Garret topped off the rally apparently in his favor with, "Well, Miss Manners, I'd say it's unanimous. We might as well give the folks what they want—kiss me."

"Aw, NOW, DON'T BE MAD," Garret said, standing outside her home's front porch screen door late that afternoon, hot sun beating down on him and his disgustingly pretty, dozen white roses.

"Mad? *Mad?*" She sort of laughed. "Oh, I passed ordinary mad a good two hours ago. At this stage, I'm immersed in boiling fury."

"Look," he said, wagging a white linen envelope addressed to her. His mother's monogram graced the flap. "I even wrote you a formal apology. That's what you wanted, right?"

"What *I* wanted," she said, her voice more shrill than she would've liked considering Lindsay was at the kitchen table doing her word definitions, "was for you to be civilized. To show the macho types of Mule Shoe that real men don't have to be afraid of manners."

"Were you even listening to some of those callers, Connie?" He devastated her fury by tugging a rose from the bouquet, stroking it down her left cheek, then right. Under her nose, enveloping her in its heady scent. His touch featherlight, he then used the rose to caress her lips. "Did you hear that guy who owned the steel fabrication shop? He wanted his men to spend time with their families—not writing notes. Tell me what's wrong with that? I wrote you this," he said, brazenly tucking the rich paper envelope into her blouse's open V. "But wouldn't my time have been better spent making tangible amends?"

"Such as…"

Heart pounding, Constance feared what he was about to do almost as much as she looked forward to it—his kiss. She knew, not because of anything he'd verbally said, but because of the way, even ten years later, she recognized the quickening in his eyes.

She wanted to stay mad at him. She wanted to stomp her feet and rail about the injustice of having her very own callers turn on her, but what he honorably hadn't mentioned was that, after the show, Felix had been so impressed by the constant stream of passionate callers, he'd given them both a thousand-dollar bonus. Garret had turned his down, offering it to her, which she'd refused. Upon arriving home, a teller from First National Bank of Mule Shoe had called. It seemed an anonymous deposit in the sum of one thousand dollars had been placed in Lindsay's college account.

"I know what you did," she said, licking her

lips, still only halfway out of the house and onto the porch. "Putting that money in Lindsay's account. I'll pay you back."

"Ironically, the only repayment I need is your thanks. Do you need my mother's address?"

"Touché."

He winked. "Just take the money, Connie. For Lindsay. It isn't much, but at least it's a start toward helping her achieve the dreams of going to college you always had."

"I'll still go," she said bristling.

"I've no doubt you will." Favoring his leg while still holding her roses, he said, "Trust me, no one hates admitting this more than me, but for today, at least, you win. Could I please crash on your couch and get a glass of water? This leg is freakin' killing me."

So much for that kiss.

Carrying Garret's water, Constance froze on the threshold between the dining room and living room to find the great Military Man sound asleep, lightly snoring.

Oh, how the mighty fall…

But then even though he was temporarily out, wasn't she the one growing more confused by the second? In the short time Garret had been back in her life, he'd turned her world upside-down.

Lindsay's meager college account could seriously use that money. But in light of the way Garret felt about Connie, the donation was outrageous. What did it mean? Was it an olive branch? If so, Constance was all the more horrible for denying him the truth. She had to tell him. But how?

"He all right?" Lindsay whispered from behind her.

"I'm sure he's just tired," Constance said. "It's been a long day." Physically, mentally and every other way in between.

"Should we call his mother and tell her he's okay?"

Resting her arm atop her wise-beyond-her-years daughter's shoulders, Constance agreed. "Where'd you learn to be such a sweetie?"

"You," Lindsay said with a swift hug and giggle before getting back to her homework.

Her child's answer was ironic, given Constance's current situation. Never had she felt less sweet! Keeping Lindsay a secret was bad enough, but then, out on the porch, she'd wanted that kiss from Garret so bad, her lips had itched. So what happened? She knew he'd been about to kiss her. What'd made him change his mind?

Assuming she'd never know, she marched into the kitchen to put her flowers in water and phone Garret's mom. Constance had expected the call to be awkward, but Mrs. Underwood was easy to talk to and seemed thankful for the update. She even complimented Constance on her portion of that afternoon's show, then apologized for her son's boorish behavior.

Upon hanging up, while Lindsay stashed her books and pencils in her backpack, then headed outside to play with her rabbits, Constance rummaged through the freezer, wondering what in the world to fix for supper. At the same time, she prayed Garret would wake up and go straight home. In the same breath, she hoped he'd be intrigued enough by the enticing scents escaping the kitchen he'd want to stay.

After finding a round steak, she popped it in the microwave to thaw, then chopped an onion. Apparently, luck was on her side as she had all the ingredients for beef Stroganoff—one of Lindsay's favorites. Would Garret enjoy the rich combination of beef, sour cream and white wine, as well?

She shouldn't care, but did.

Speaking of the devil... A noise in the living room made her glance over her shoulder to find Garret hobbling her way.

"Mmm...something smells good."

"You're welcome to stay," she somehow managed to say.

"Cool. Let me call Mom."

"I, um, already did—not to tell her you'd be staying for dinner, just that you'd fallen asleep on my sofa."

"How sweet of you."

There was that word again. "It, um, was actually Lindsay's idea."

"She's a cutie," he said, easing onto one of the kitchen table's maple chairs. "Nathan must be even more of an oaf than I'd imagined not to want to be with her every chance he gets."

"Stop it with the Nathan bashing. He's busy," Constance said, back at the stove, stirring, wondering what had stopped her from booting Garret out the door.

"That's a cop-out excuse. Why are you protecting him all the time?"

"I protect Nathan because he's a good guy. He spends lots of time with Lindsay. As for financial support, he offers money all the time. I don't want it."

"Then how come you accepted my gift for Lindsay?"

Great question.

One she had absolutely no answer for. If she were consistent with her making-it-on-my-own rule, then she'd have politely returned the gift. Why, why hadn't she? Surely not because Garret was Lindsay's dad? And as such, the sentimental value had been worth far more than the money itself?

Garret shot her a look that could only be utter contempt. It shocked her how badly his disapproval hurt. Still, she held her chin high and her stare locked with his. There was no backing down now—not if she didn't want her daughter carried off halfway across the world. Pushing himself up from the table, he braced himself, then set off hobbling toward the door.

"Where are you going?"

"Home. I'm no longer hungry."

"What don't you get about the fact that this is *my* life, Garret? Remember how I told you about what happened with my dad when I was little? Please, try to understand, I can't—won't—have Lindsay going through the same pain."

"You're honestly afraid Nathan's going to take her from you?"

Crossing her fingers behind her back, praying for forgiveness for her ever-deepening lies, she nodded. It was best Garret left. Thanks to Felix, they were being forced together at work, but having him here—at home—was far too dangerous.

The back door crashed open. Lindsay hurried through, cheeks sweaty and flushed, smile brighter than the sun. "Got everybody fed and watered. I played with the bunnies for a while, but I'm really hungry. Dinner almost done?"

"Just about, sweetie." Constance gripped her

daughter in a desperate hug. "Go wash up and I'll set the table."

"'Kay." On her way out of the kitchen, to Garret she said, "Mom's Stroganoff is the best. Promise you'll like it."

"I'm sure I will," he said, "but will there be ice cream for dessert?"

"Hopefully lots," the girl said with a giggle before running off.

"Thought you were leaving?" Constance reminded, heart pounding.

Head bowed, he fell back into his chair. "Sorry. My constant need to save the world is a problem I need to work out."

"I don't follow."

Cradling his forehead, he said, "I've seen a lot of things. Inherently wrong, vile, sins-against-God-and-nature kinds of things. Injustice pisses me off on a level I've never seemed able to get a grip on." Looking up, eyes red he shook his head. "You and Lindsay don't have a financial pot to piss in—pardon my French—yet she seems incredibly happy and well-adjusted. When you let down your guard, you do, too. All the money in the world's not going to change that, and yet I can't seem to keep my nose out of your affairs. That's what I'm sorry about."

Relief shimmering through her, Constance

exhaled sharply, then wrapped her arms around Garret in a warm hug. "Thank you for understanding. For agreeing to let it go. Despite what you think, Nathan's a wonderful man and, um, father. He loves Lindsay very much. It's just that because of what happened to me, I have this sense that I can never be too careful."

"For the record," he said, his voice gruff, "I ever come across that prick in a dark alley, he's going down."

She winced. "Language."

"Give me a break," he said, once she'd headed back to the stove to ladle their meal into a serving bowl. "Can you honestly think of a polite way to describe him?"

"Yes. As my friend. He's as sorry as I am for what happened when we were younger, and—"

"I'm starving," Lindsay said. "Want me to set the table?"

"Please," Constance said over the clatter of her daughter already yanking the dish cabinet door open, then gathering three plates.

"Anything I can do to help?" Garret asked, wondering at the efficiency flowing between mother and daughter. He hadn't considered the fact that Constance might actually fear reprisal from her ex. Garret might've told Constance he'd let it go, but before leaving for Virginia, one way or another, he'd find out what was really going on.

"Garret, you'd better just sit," Lindsay directed with the concerned tone of a little nurse.

Constance laughed. "I concur. We can't have you falling asleep at the table."

"Sorry about that," he said with a chuckle. "Sometimes this da—bum leg of mine hurts more than my pride likes to admit."

"It's okay to say you're hurt," Lindsay said, setting his plate in front of him, then a bundle of napkins and silverware. "Otherwise, how will anyone know you need help?"

"From the mouths of babes," he mumbled, sharing a look with the girl's mother.

Constance set the food on the table and then they were off, sharing a meal like the real family he'd once invested all of himself into wanting.

He still did want a family all his own with a sometimes fierce longing, but his line of work was one you didn't just up and quit. Sure, guys on his team had wives and kids, but secretly, Garret had often thought they were irresponsible. Make no mistake, every mission they embarked upon, no one planned on returning home in a pine box. But it happened. If Garret were ever fortunate enough to be given the gift of a woman's love, then a child's, he wasn't sure he could bear leaving them, perhaps not to come back. Sure, he could just as easily take a factory job and die in a machinery accident. Or even be a lawyer like his dad and suffer a heart attack behind his desk. But to carry on as a SEAL seemed like asking for trouble. In his experience, fate had a funny way of screwing with you—just when you started to feel safe was when most things went wrong.

"That was delicious," Garret said when he was done.

"Told you," Lindsay said.

"That you did." Returning her grin, he ruffled her hair, wondering at the downy softness. He couldn't remember the last time he'd touched a child. But this…it somehow felt different as if his history with Constance gave him a stake in the girl's well-being. Ridiculous, seeing how he hardly knew her, but he couldn't help what he felt, and so he went with it, thoroughly enjoying every aspect of the night.

After dinner, leaning against the counter, Garret dried while Constance washed. Along with Constance, he helped Lindsay practice lines for an upcoming school performance of *Red Riding in the Hood*—only, instead of the big, bad wolf, Red encountered numerous unsavoury characters representing smoking, gangs and drugs. Again, the warrior lurking within him rose, wanting to protect this child—and her mother—from the big, bad world.

Constance announced Lindsay's bedtime and, after a few obligatory grumbles he'd have expected from a girl her age, she wrapped her mom in a fierce hug, then him.

"Thanks for helping with my lines," she said, enveloping him in her little girl sweetness. Or maybe it was the apple cobbler à la mode she'd spilled on her red T-shirt during dinner. Either way, her gesture deeply touched him.

"You're welcome," he said past a surprising knot in his throat. Something about the kid tugged at his heart. He felt connected to her. Stupid, but there it was.

Constance excused herself to tuck in the girl.

Alone on the same sofa he'd earlier conked out on, in the sparsely furnished living room with its ancient TV and threadbare, lumpy furniture, Garret thought of plenty he'd like to change about the place, but despite its shabby appearance, there was no mistaking the house's love. The realization made him not want to change a thing, but rather be a part of it.

He led a full, exhilarating life in Virginia, but on those nights when he was alone in his condo, listening to the faint sounds of lives going on around him, the snippets of laughter next door, or the father and son living above him who playfully wrestled like a herd of stampeding buffalo, he wondered.

What would it be like to share his life with someone? Which inevitably led him back to that brief, shining time with Constance, as she was the only woman to ever breach the loneliness in his soul.

And then she was back, flooding the room with her warm, breathy laugh. "Judging by how long Lindsay brushed and brushed and brushed her teeth, she didn't want to go to bed."

"I remember pulling that stunt," he said, joining in her laughter.

She parked beside him, patting his thigh. "Seriously, thanks for your help with those lines. Lindsay always giggles when I deliver the tough guy lines. You added so much realism, you might have a second career in acting."

"Good to know," he said, covering her hand with his. "In case the Navy should ever decide to let me go."

As if only just now realizing where she'd placed her hand, she moved it, but he held fast to her slim, cool fingers. "This has been a nice night. I should be the one thanking you."

A faint smile tugged the corners of her lips. "How about thanking me on air tomorrow by behaving?"

"Aw, now," he said, leaning into her, nudging her shoulder, "where would the fun be in that?"

She snatched a green corduroy throw pillow, tackling him with it. "The fun would be in actually being able to breathe since I wouldn't be afraid of what you're about to say next."

"Breathing's highly overrated," he teased, still holding her hand. Her fingers had warmed. He'd done that, given her this small bit of comfort. Yet why should he care? She'd hurt him worse than the fall that'd broken his leg.

"What do you suggest as a replacement?"

"To breathing?"

His own breath hitched as he once again found himself in the torturous position of wanting—no, *having*—to kiss her. "Best replacement I know, is this…."

The distance between them was penetrated in a heartbeat. Her lips were hot, moist. And when, by mutual consent, their lips parted and he commenced with stroking her tongue, an overwhelming sense of coming home flooded his soul. Her breath was indescribably, deliciously laced with after-dinner coffee. Even awkwardly perched beside him on the sofa, her lush curves gave purpose to his strength.

Hands cupping her face, smoothing her hair, he kissed her, kissed her till she was moaning. This was wrong. Kissing her, holding her, wanting her worse than life. Wrong, because she'd hurt him once and would only do it again. A fiercely independent woman, Constance didn't need a man in her life.

So then what am I doing here?

"My God..." she said, once he'd drawn away. Pressing trembling fingers to her lips, she shook her head, then smiled. "I feel transported in time."

"That's your second serving of cobbler talking through indigestion."

"No," she said with a firm shake of her head. "Garret, what have you done to me? That kiss. Didn't you—if only for an instant—get the feeling things never changed between us?"

Yes. Trouble was, everything had changed. Nowhere near for the better.

"I should get going," he said. "It's late. What time do you want me back in the morning to help plan the next show?"

"Garret?"

He pushed himself up from the sofa.

"Everything okay?" Her gaze followed him as he hobbled across the room.

"Sure," he said. "Why wouldn't it be?"

She lightly shook her head, touched her brows. "Did I miss something? Literally, a few seconds ago, we were connecting on a level I never thought possible, yet now..."

"I have to go," he said. "Mom will be worried."

"Of course. But still..."

"I'm just trying to be considerate. Isn't that what you'd do?" His sarcastic tone was accidental. One that'd cropped up right when he knew falling for her all over again could be the worst mistake of his life.

"Whoa," she said, struggling to her feet, striding to where he stood beneath the entry hall arch. "How dare you speak to me about consideration? I just—"

"You just had the audacity to sit there, crooning about how it felt like things have never changed between us, yet right upstairs," he spat in a stage whisper, "is a child you had by another man. A child—to the best of my calculations, you could've conceived with me. So pardon if I don't get warm and fuzzy tripping down Memory Lane."

Though she visibly trembled under his verbal attack, he was powerless to comfort her, seeing how giving voice to his suspicion that she'd been sleeping with Nathan at the same time as him made Garret's stomach roil. He'd loved her. Loved her with frightening intensity. He'd been so damned certain she'd loved him back. How could she have betrayed him that way?

"For the record," she said, her voice hollow and shaded with infinite levels of pain. "I *never* slept with Nathan until after we'd already broken up."

"I'm not dumb, Connie. I did pretty well in math."

"How'd you do in med school? Lindsay was born premature. It happens."

"You exhaust me, having a ready-made excuse for all occasions. Why, for once, can't you just say, 'Garret, I screwed up. Sorry.'"

"I don't say that word."

"Screwed?" he said with a brittle laugh. "Or sorry?"

"Get out," she said, tears shimmering in her eyes. "Get out and stay out. You're no longer welcome in my home."

"Great." Sounded like a fine solution to him. Now the only problem was, how did he get the woman out of his heart?

Chapter Seven

"You all right?" Renee-Marie asked Connie the next day, twenty minutes before going on air. They were in the broadcast booth, each holding steaming mugs of Lemon Zinger tea. From out on the street came the annoying chomp of a road crew's jackhammers. Constance hoped with the soundproof door closed, the noise would lessen. "You look like you spent the night wrestling a gator and the gator won."

"Be sure and add psychic to your résumé, seeing how you pegged how I feel."

After a sip of tea, Renee-Marie asked, "Was it a big gator or little?"

"Big."

"Ahh…" she said with a nod. "The Military Man?"

"Ding, ding, ding," Constance said. "Right again."

Renee-Marie shook her head. "I hate what Felix

is making you do, but on the flip side, just think how exciting it would be for you to have the top-rated show in the state!"

Embracing her friend in a warm hug, wishing she could ease herself into a steaming tub to erase kinks left by Garret's amazing kisses, Constance sighed. "I always thought that was what I wanted, but at what price?"

"Only you can decide that," Renee-Marie said with a sympathetic cluck.

A knock sounded on the open door.

The instant Constance looked up, it felt as if the air had been sucked from the room. Garret's presence was all-consuming, larger than life. During their kiss, she'd felt, if only for a moment, in peril of once more drowning in his spell. It would be so easy to fall for him again. He might've grown up in Mule Shoe, just like her, but he wasn't from her world—not really. He had goals and dreams and talents that had gotten him far away from here. Just as he'd left for basic training, he'd leave this time just as soon as his leg healed. Even worse, after their most recent exchange of words, it was obvious he still carried a boatload of animosity where their history was concerned.

In her heart of hearts, Constance knew she'd never cheated on Garret—not even when she'd married Nathan. Garret had been the only man for her—ever. Which only made the distance between them that much harder to bear.

And that much more crucial to maintain.

"Renee-Marie," Garret said, "think we could have a moment alone?"

"Depends," the fiery Cajun said. "What do you have to say? Miss Manners is upset enough."

"I'm fine," Constance said, touched by her friend's protective streak. "Really. But, thanks."

Renee-Marie patted her back, shot her cohost a scathing glare, then left, shutting the door behind her.

"I have nothing to say to you." Constance approached her chair, straightening her notes in preparation for the afternoon's broadcast.

"I have plenty to say to you."

"Yeah, well, you might want to hurry, seeing how we're on air in ten minutes."

"Look at me," he said, snagging her by her upper arm, tugging her close.

"I don't want to look at you. I don't want to be anywhere near you. Were it not for my boss, I wouldn't be with you now."

"Dammit, woman, I'm trying to explain, but you do something to me I can't—" Raking his fingers through his hair, he said, "Never mind. Let's just do the show."

"Horace," Renee-Marie said two hours later, "from Ponca City's on line four."

"Thank you, Horace," Constance said, refusing to make eye contact with her cohost, "for joining us. As a gentle reminder, today's topic is Finger Foods—Delicious Treats or Etiquette Traps?"

"*I vote traps,*" Horace said with conviction. "*I was on a first date with my wife at a steak place when she starts eating fries with her fork. Well, I'd already dug in with my fingers when she gives me this look. The rest of the night she was uptight. Took me five years of dating before she'd finally marry me.*"

"Man," Garret said, "I feel your pain on that. And so you think just eating those stupid fries with a fork would've fast-tracked you to wedded bliss?"

"*Nah...*" Horace laughed. "*Finger foods weren't my only bad habit. I left the toilet seat up, belched at the table and accidentally ran out of gas at Lover's Bluff.*"

"So?" Constance asked, "for love, did you straighten up and get a better grasp on rudimentary etiquette?"

The caller laughed again, this time so hard he snorted. "*Heck no. She just finally gave in to the realization that she could love me or leave me, but there sure wasn't hope of fixin' me. We've been together fifty-five years come June.*"

"Congratulations, man," Garret said. "I'm glad your story had a happy ending."

"Wait just a minute," Constance interjected.

"How is it good that Horace's poor wife had to abandon her standards?"

"She got a great man, didn't she? If you love someone, shouldn't you be willing to overlook a few flaws?"

"Like you were last night?" The instant the words left her mouth, Constance knew she'd messed up. Not only did the phone lines light up, but Garret's expression settled into a mask of fury.

"You really want to go there?" he asked, his voice lethally low.

Renee-Marie momentarily defused the public portion of the altercation by piping in with, "Here's the latest from Big Hal's Tires, where coffee and conversation are always free." To Constance she said via the booth's private intercom, "I bought you five minutes. What you two do with them is your business." She turned her back to them, burying her head in her new copy of *People*.

"Sorry," Constance gushed. "I never meant to say that on air. It just slipped out."

"Connie, we seriously can't go on like this."

"I know. I feel awful."

"About what?" he asked, staring uncomfortably deep into her eyes. "What you did with Nathan? That you got caught? Or—"

"Everything," she said, doubling over in her chair, kneading throbbing temples. "I'm sorry about everything, okay? But mostly, that I ever let you go."

"What?" Wheeling his chair closer, he eased his fingers under her chin, forcing her to meet his gaze. "What in Sam Hill's that mean? You *let* me go?"

"I don't know what I mean," she said, covering her face with her hands. "Let's forget I ever said it, okay?"

"No, it's seriously not okay. You can't just throw something like that out there, then—"

"Great show, guys!" Felix tossed open the door so hard it banged against the opposing wall. "You two are spinning airwaves into gold. And I don't want to get your hopes up, but there's been so much buzz about you two, WKOK out of Oklahoma City is considering picking up the show."

"It's not for sale," Garret said. "Now if you don't mind, please step out…or I'll throw you out."

"WE NEED TO TALK," Garret shouted after the show, chasing Connie through the station's blistering lot. Out front, the jackhammers were doing their thing. Heat undulated in shimmering waves off the blacktop. Garret paused, raising the hem of his white golf shirt to wipe his brow.

"I have to get home to meet Lindsay's bus."

"In over an hour."

"I have housework to do."

"Fine," he said. "We'll talk at the house."

"I'd rather not."

"Woman, what don't you get about the fact that I'm doing you the favor? Why are you always giving me such grief?"

He'd finally reached her car, where she'd already climbed inside. She put the key in the ignition, but got nothing from the engine but a *ruh, ruh, ruh.*

"Why?" she railed, fisting the wheel.

"Pop the hood and I'll give you a jump."

Constance did as he'd asked and within a few minutes, her car had started and she was on her way home, Garret tailing her—according to him, in case her car quit again.

She made it home safely, and while her car seemed fine, she was having a devil of a time trying not to hyperventilate.

Pulling alongside the house, she creaked open her car door, then stepped into blazing sun, dry heat and a stiff breeze that did nothing for her allergies or mood.

She sneezed.

Garret pulled his mother's Caddie into her gravel drive, only stirring more dust.

Next time she sneezed, he was right beside her. "Bless you."

"Thanks." She tilted her face to the sun and scooped her hair into a makeshift bun, wishing she'd worn it up in the first place.

The breeze cooled her sweaty nape, if only for an instant, providing the illusion of comfort.

Personally, she thought her hair felt and looked better up, which was why she'd worn it down—not wanting to appear to have expended the slightest effort on her appearance.

Oh, that makes a lot of sense, her conscience interjected, seeing how only a few days earlier, Garret had remarked how he preferred she wear her hair down.

"Lindsay gets home around four, right?"

Dropping her hair, which she'd lifted to cool her sweaty nape, Constance sighed, then nodded.

"Good. I want this off the conversational table before she gets here."

Hot dread of another argument bothered her far more than unseasonably warm weather. "We've been over everything. You're not attracted to me. I'm not attracted to you. You've been kind enough to stick by me for the sake of my job, and yet I've been an inconsiderate wench. Blah, blah, blah. Doesn't that sum it up?" Not waiting for his answer, she mounted the back porch steps. Easing the key into the door, she stepped into the mercifully cool, dark kitchen.

Her uninvited guest barged past her, nearly knocking her over to lean on a chair. Eyeing her fridge, he asked, "Got beer?"

"No."

"Hard stuff?"

After slamming the back door, she faced him, hands on her hips.

"Should I take that as a no?"

"I can barely afford electric, so why would I waste money on booze other than to use it for cooking?"

"Didn't you get the memo?" he asked, helping himself to a glass from the cabinet, filling it with water, then taking a couple deep swigs. "If you drink enough, the lights go on without electric." He winked. "SEAL humor."

She groaned. Not from his awful joke, but the sight of him. Standing on one leg, the man still managed to exude power. Dark hair now rakishly overgrown, sweat damp at the temples. Even darker eyes closed, savoring the water as if it were nectar.

"H-how long are you planning to stay?" she asked.

"Well…" He peered out the kitchen sink window. "Right after we talk, I thought I might fix that broken front porch shutter."

"Not necessary."

"Call it basic human decency."

"You limp when you walk. How are you going to get up on a ladder?"

"I have skills."

Grabbing her own water, she forced herself to

ask, "Seeing how most of our *discussions* seem to take a while, whatever topic's burning your tongue, you might want to get started."

"Okay… It seems I have a problem—or maybe we both have a problem." He shrugged. "At the moment, I can't really tell."

"I'll bite. What does this problem entail?"

"It's complex. Multifaceted. Demands a three-sided attack."

"Oh?" There he was again, making her heart race with just that hooded look forewarning a kiss—or, at least it used to. Now, she wasn't sure what it preceded, just that usually, she was the one reeling from the aftereffects.

"One…" he said, hobbling closer. "Two…" he slipped his hand under the fall of her hair, tugging her against him.

"Why do I get the feeling I'm not going to like three?" She shivered as sweat evaporated from her neck, only to be warmed by his fingers' brush. Though her lips tingled in anticipation of another kiss, she knew how detrimental that lip-lock would be to the secrets she'd sworn to forever keep.

"Oh," he said, kissing her upper lip with a breathy laugh, "I think you'll like it just fine."

"Promise?" It was a silly question. Even more silly was the notion she cared. But as he touched his lips to hers with the slightest hint of pressure, only deepening the kiss when she'd encouraged him with a moan, she found she cared very much. Knees weak, stomach knotted with tentative delight, she found herself wanting more—no, make that *all*—of Garret.

"Well?" he asked, leaning back with a cocky grin. "Did I make good on that promise?"

Despite herself, she lurched a step forward, clinging to him, pressing her cheek against his chest, oddly reassured to find his heart pounding as heavily as hers. "You asked last night if I knew the word *sorry,* and I do, Garret. You'll never know how sorry I am that I ever put Nathan between us. You have to know I never meant to hurt you."

Backing her up, framing her face with his hands, he asked, "Then why did you?"

"I can't say."

"Can't or won't?"

"Hi, Mom! Hi, Garret!" Lindsay shouted on her way through the back door. As usual, she was breathless from running and her cheeks were flushed.

Constance backed up, out of Garret's hold, but apparently, she hadn't been fast enough. "Lindsay? What're you doing home early?"

"*Euw,*" her daughter said. "Emily's mom was at school, helping get ready for Pizza Bingo Night, so she took me and Em home so we wouldn't have to ride the bus." After making another face that looked as if she'd just eaten a night crawler, she asked, "You guys dating?"

"Would that be a bad thing?" Garret asked.

"I thought you were dating Miss Calloway?"

"We went out for coffee. And, keep this on the down low, but I'm pretty sure she has a thing for your gym teacher and was using me to make him jealous."

"Really?" Lindsay asked, eyebrows raised. "I've gotta call Emily and Julie."

"Hey," Constance hollered while Lindsay made a mad dash for the living room phone. "What did Garret just say about not blabbing this private info about your teacher?"

"But…"

"Lindsay…"

"Oh, all right." She grabbed honey mustard pretzels and a boxed apple juice from the pantry, then said, "If you need me, I'll be doing my homework with my rabbits."

"Love you," Constance called after her.

"Uh-huh." Lindsay let the screen door slam behind her with all the moody flair of a budding preteen.

"Guess she told you," Garret said, smile playing about his lips.

"Yep, I feel suitably dissed."

"I don't mean to get back into your business where she's concerned, but is it hard raising her alone?"

"I do okay," Constance said, leaving him to forage in the freezer more to escape his intense stare than because she was in any particular hurry to start dinner. "Actually, it's only been the past year or so since I've had any discipline problems from her—and then, it was only sass. Nothing I couldn't handle."

Garret pulled out a chair at the table and eased onto it. "What happens when she hits her terrible teens? Got a battle plan?"

Aha—drumsticks. She thumped the frozen mass onto the counter where it sounded more like bricks than dinner.

"Connie? Got a plan?"

Hands back on her hips, she sighed. "No, Mr. Expert Parent, I have no plan—unless winging it counts."

"Ouch. I just asked a simple question."

"And I gave you a simple answer." After popping the drumsticks in the microwave, then setting the defrost cycle, she leaned against the counter, arms crossed.

"What's for dinner?"

"Fried chicken."

"Am I invited?"

Moaning, covering her face with her hands, she said, "Why would you even want to be invited?"

His naughty-boy grin licked the same spot in her belly as his kisses. "You still owe me a straight answer about Nathan. If I stay, I figure I can get that, plus a good meal."

"What about your mom?"

"She's at a church meeting, then riding with a friend to some candle outlet to buy candles for church. Told me at breakfast I'd have to get my own dinner."

"GET IT?" GARRET ASKED Lindsay an hour later about the homework math problems she'd been stuck on. She'd spread her books and papers across the living room coffee table, and sat cross-legged on the floor, while he perched on the sofa's edge with his bum leg cocked at a crazy angle. Though his doc assured him it was healing fine, when it ached like this, Garret couldn't help but worry. As if he didn't already have enough on his plate without dealing with whether or not he'd ever again be physically strong enough to handle his job.

Amazing smells floated from the kitchen, along with Connie's off-key humming. Whereas just knowing she was five yards away normally churned his guts, tonight, her presence—and Lindsay's—felt oddly comforting.

"I think I understand," Lindsay said with a nod. "But I'm afraid by the time I get to school tomorrow, I'll get it all messed up in my head."

"Just think of it in terms of pizza slices and it works every time."

"Yeah, but—" she scrunched her button nose

"—what if it's one of those where the numbers are bigger than the pizza?"

"Doesn't matter," he said, fighting the craziest urge to give an affectionate tug on her nearest pigtail. "Just draw out bigger pizzas till you get the hang of it."

"Okay. Thanks. Can I go play hide-and-seek with Sarah and her brother?"

"You'd have to ask your mom on that."

"Mommmm!"

Garret winced. Who knew such a small body housed such a huge banshee wail?

Once Lindsay had run off to be with her friends, knowing she had to be home in an hour, Garret was back in the kitchen, shoulder against the wall beside the fridge, watching his former girl work her magic. "I remember," he said with a chuckle, "when you couldn't even bake Christmas cookies without burning them or overworking the dough." He shook his head in amazement at the appetizing spread taking form. "Look at you now."

"I'm pushing thirty," she said, wiping her hands on a frilly white apron. Was it wrong to want to see her wearing it *sans* the jeans and T-shirt she'd changed into? "Isn't it about time I learned to cook?"

"Well, sure, but from the sounds of it, you haven't yet learned to sing, so…"

"Creep!" She tossed a dishrag at him, which he easily caught.

"Connie," he said, turning serious. "Back there with Lindsay, I kept getting the feeling I've known her forever. Kind of the way I feel around you but different. Protective. And when we ran over her lines for the play the other day, I found myself resenting my job because odds are, I won't be here to see her perform."

"I'm no expert," Constance said, fully aware she was meandering down a conversational path littered with land mines. "But it seems to me you're just transferring what remains of your feelings for me onto her."

No way could it be genetics giving you that bond.

"Yeah," he said, hobbling to the table to take a seat. "You're probably right. Before meeting Lindsay, I never thought all that much about kids, after spending time with her, they seem fun."

"It's not all fun," she offered, thrilled he'd put more distance between them. "Those early years were tough. And when you have to ask fifteen times to get the trash taken out, that gets old."

"Sure. Still, I'm just saying, maybe one of these days I should at least think about settling down. I'm not getting any younger."

"Puh-lease," she said, turning the meat, wincing when hot oil splattered her forearm. "You've got all the time in the world."

"Do I?" he asked from her side, lifting her wound to his lips, kissing away the sting.

"Of course you do." Disconcerted to say the least, she yanked back her arm. "Once you return to Virginia, you'll go on a few more missions, doing whatever it is you do. Then, one night, while you're out carousing at some bar, you'll—"

"Carousing?"

"Isn't that what you G.I. Joe types do after hours?"

"Sometimes," he said. "But the body can't take it like it used to."

Really? Because judging from where she stood, his body was fine! Licking her lips, she said, "I'm sorry to hear that."

"Are you, Connie?" He took one wrist captive, then the other, kissing them in turn. "Really sorry? Or is that just lip service, the way you talk about being sorry about what went down with Nathan?"

"How do you do that?" she said, flustered by the sudden roar of her pulse.

"What?"

"That mental wrestling move where one minute, we're standing peacefully in the center of the ring, then whomp, you've kicked my feet out from under me, and you've got me conversationally pinned."

"That what I did?"

"You know full well that's what you did, or you wouldn't be wearing that satisfied smirk." She tried wrenching free, but failed. Oh, he might look helpless and weak with his limp, but the man's arms were velvet traps. Even in his current condition, she had no doubt he could easily take out an entire platoon, so why should she for one minute think she'd be safe beside him?

"So now I smirk, too?"

"You're maddening."

"You're beautiful." Just like that, he'd pinned her again, kissing her, sweeping his hands in long, lovely arcs up her back. Creating an atmospheric time capsule winging her back to the past, fogging her brain and resolve to steer clear of him till she found herself actually clinging to him. She'd spent hours kissing him, teasing him, flirting with him when they'd been kids. She could easily do it again now. But what then? What if all of this kissing was a smoke screen cleverly devised to get to the truth about Lindsay's paternity? God only knew what mercenary mind games Garret had been trained in.

"Daaammmn," he softly said, drawing back. With the pad of his thumb, he brushed her swollen lips. "Hey? What's with the basset hound expression?"

"I'm good," she said with a firm shake of her head. "So is your kissing. Just leads me down the path of what might've been."

"Yeah…" Resting his forehead against hers, he laughed. "I know what you mean. Been there myself more than a few times since we've hooked back up."

"Is that what we've done, Garret?"

"Damned if I know. When you kiss me like that, making those little moaning noises, I'm pretty much a goner."

"Really?" she asked. "Or are you just saying that?" *Just trying to make me believe you care, when all the while, you're setting me up for a nasty, revenge-themed fall?*

"If you think I'm playing games with you, you're wrong. I don't know what went down between you and Nathan—I hope one day you'll trust me enough to tell me—but in the here and now, wanting you so bad, I'm finding all that really matters is getting back into your good graces." He kissed her again. Kissed her with a soft, sweet completeness she'd thought forever lost. "And not repeating past mistakes."

Did he even know what he was saying? Heat and unbearable, shimmering hope sang through her until she was actually trembling from the force of giddy relief. Of course, he wasn't here to steal Lindsay. That was her ugly past rearing its suspicious head.

Trouble was, considering the magnitude of the secret she held tight, she wasn't any more worthy of him now than she'd been back then.

Chapter Eight

"Garret!" Connie hollered up at him from where she stood in the front yard, hands on her hips, giving him that supposed fierce look he'd learned in the past four days to kiss right off her face. "Come down from the roof right now before you get hurt."

"My leg's already mostly healed and has a steel rod running through it!" he shouted while hammering another new shingle. "If I fall, what's the worst that can happen?"

"You break the other one!"

He waved her off and kept right on hammering. Lord, but it felt good being useful again. Felt even better being back with his girl. Granted, there'd been nothing official said between them, but since their talk over frying chicken, there'd been a subtle change even his mother had noticed. Their on-air battles were still heated, but no blood was spilled.

And their kisses… If they didn't get a chance to take things further soon, he'd explode. Which was why he was now perched on a sweltering roof after an already grueling day.

Hmm… With Lindsay at a friend's practicing lines and not due home till after supper, what was he doing up here on the roof when he could be working his way into Connie's bedroom? Sure, with him soon returning to Virginia, and too many unresolved issues between them, bed was the last place they needed to be. But even knowing all that did nothing to stop the wanting.

The aluminum ladder's metallic jiggle alerted him that he'd soon have company. "Garret," Connie complained, poking that pretty head of hers just above the gutter, "I really wish you'd get down from there. My roof has happily leaked for five years. Why this sudden compulsion for you to fix it today?"

"It's supposed to rain all day tomorrow."

"Yes, that occasionally happens around here."

"Well? Do you want your ceilings to cave in?"

"No, but—"

"Woman, quit being contrary. I've got this handled. Or are you up here wanting to help?"

"Me? Help fix the roof?" Eyes huge, she surveyed the gabled slope. To him, it didn't seem all that steep.

"Heck, yeah. Get those sweet buns up here and hand me another shingle."

Though it took her a good five minutes to crawl cautiously on all fours beside him, by the time she'd made it, he was as tickled by the proud smile on her face as she was. "Wow, look at this view…."

"See? Roofing's not all that bad, is it?" Unless, of course, you happened to be in his shoes, seated beside a rooftop goddess whose deceptively simple white T-shirt was soaked with sweat and showing a tad more of her blue-and-white-polka-dotted bra than was probably proper. Her complexion glowed from the heat, making it official—she was the most gorgeous roofer in all of Oklahoma.

"Gimme the hammer," she said, shingle already in hand. "What do I do?"

He positioned it for her, handed her nails, then let her pound away.

"This is fun," she said. "Hand me another."

"Hey," he teasingly complained, "I thought you were supposed to be assisting me?"

She stuck out her tongue while he did her bidding.

Working in tandem, they'd soon finished the job and were seated on the rickety old yard swing, surveying their work.

"You're a mess," Connie said, eyeing his sweaty, grimy forearms and frayed jeans.

"Tell me something I don't know," he said with a laugh.

"So how are we going to get you cleaned up?"

"We?" Easing his arm around her shoulders, he raised his eyebrows, then shot her a lazy grin. "I like the sound of that."

"Have you no shame?" she asked, at least attempting to sound coy, even though her body betrayed what he hoped were her true feelings by the way she'd leaned into his hold.

"Nah." He had no trouble hefting her onto his lap for a lingering kiss. What he did have trouble with was knowing he should probably keep his hands off. In a few weeks, he'd be heading home, then what? He'd be lying if he said he didn't want to be with her every day for the rest of his life, but it wasn't that simple. There was pride involved over what'd gone down between her and Nathan. He had commitments well over a thousand miles away. She had a kid who might not take kindly to suddenly having a new father. So why was it that at the moment, none of those obstacles seemed to matter? "No shame at all. Just hunger."

"Hunger, huh?" She kissed him, nipping his lower lip. "Lindsay won't be home for hours. How about we get cleaned up, then I'll make you supper."

"No good." He shook his head. "It's not that kind of hunger." Staring at her straight on, making sure there were no misunderstandings, he said as plainly as he knew how, "I want to make love to you, Connie."

"I'd like that, too, but…"

"What's wrong?" He didn't like the doubt shadowing her expression.

"Wouldn't we be moving too fast?"

"Too fast?" He snorted. "Baby, we've done it before."

"There's more at stake now," she said, worrying her lower lip. "Back then, we had nothing better to do. But now, there are bills to pay and laundry needing to be done and—"

Fingers on her chin, he said, "Drop the BS and tell me what's really on your mind."

"O-okay. You'll soon be gone. Then what? I—I can't believe I'm even saying this, but…" She took her hands from his chest to slide them into her hair. "Having you here again, it's been like some crazy, cosmic do-over. But it's not real. Can't you see that? I mean, I'm sitting here with you in the beautiful sun, falling for you all over again, only twice as hard, and yet—"

"Stop," he said, cradling her face with his hands. "I'm scared, too. There's a lot we need to work out. But this…" He kissed her again. "Has always worked fine. Let's go with the moment, see where it leads."

"See where it leads?" Her scattered laugh sounded borderline hysterical. Scrambling from his lap to pace the patchy grass in front of the swing, her hands were back at her forehead. "What am I doing? I'm a parent. I can't just run around indulging in wild flings."

In a heartbeat he stood behind her, hands looped around her waist. "This wouldn't be like that."

"What would it be like then? Newsflash, Garret, your leg won't hurt forever. You lead a wildly exciting life I can only dream of. There's never been the slightest thing holding a man like you to a town like Mule Shoe."

"That's where you're wrong," he said, kissing her nose, searching her deep blue stare. "More than I could've imagined. You're holding me here. I don't have a clue where this thing between us is going. Truthfully, I'm still mad at you, but also mad for you. Lord help me, but I'm falling for you all over again."

"No, no, no," she said, all the while smoothing her hands across his chest. "You mustn't say things like that."

"Why not?"

"B-because I lost you once and it nearly destroyed me. How am I supposed to be with you in every way a man and woman can, then say goodbye? And Lindsay—she's already becoming attached to you, and—"

"And that's a bad thing, why? Christ, Connie, as usual, you're overanalyzing the situation. Right now, this very minute, walk upstairs with me. We'll share a shower, a few kisses, then see where it leads." *I might've spent the last decade stuck in the past, but by god, I'm not willing to stay there one more day. I'm sick of pining for what could've been when right here—now—I can reclaim the one woman I never should've let go.* "We don't have to decide the next ten years of our lives—" he brushed her lips with his "—just the next ten minutes."

CONSTANCE'S SKIN felt oddly supercharged, as if the water streaming from the shower were alive— or maybe it was herself coming alive for the first time since Garret had been gone.

"You're beautiful," he said, standing behind her, kissing her shoulder with his hands around her waist.

"Mmm…" Leaning against him, she murmured, "You, too." At first, she'd felt self-conscious being naked in front of him, but like everything else about their reunion, it had come as naturally as kissing. Being in his arms again was nothing short of a miracle. Yet with her secret still between them, her pleasure was nowhere near complete.

Garret spun her to face him, cinched her close.

"Be careful. You could slip and get hurt."

He shrugged. "If I fall, I've got you to catch me."

He was right, which was why she angled in the water to make room for him, easing her arms around him, loving his slick, hard feel against her. "I've missed you," she said so softly she couldn't be sure she'd spoken at all.

He kissed the top of her head, holding her beneath the spray until the water turned cold and then laughing, shivering, they helped each other out only to take their time toweling each other dry.

She led him to the bed, letting him use her as a crutch. With more laughing, they finally made it to the girly, wrought-iron affair she'd never shared with anyone other than her daughter on occasional nights after she'd had a bad dream.

"What's this?" he asked, fingering the tiny brass key she wore on a fine gold chain around her neck.

"It's the key to my heart," she teased, unable to tell him the key's true significance. Maybe she would in time. But definitely not now.

"Mmm…" he said with more kisses. "Interesting."

"Not really," she said, itching to drop the subject.

"Too bad." He winked before dousing her in more kisses, succeeding in making her want him that much more.

Garret's injured leg wasn't making their efforts to take things to the next level easy. While he made a brave front at being fine, his subtle winces told her it still hurt. "Didn't your doctor give you tips on how to—you know—so that your leg doesn't hurt?"

"Gee," he said, sitting back on his elbows, "seeing how when I left the hospital, it was with the intent to hang with my mother for a few months, sex wasn't the first thing on my mind."

"Well…" she said, noticing how he was pretty much spread like a masculine buffet before her, then taking advantage of the fact by kissing a trail down his abs. Was it wrong for her to revel in girl power when certain portions of his anatomy began to grow? "I suppose we'll just have to abandon this mission and try again once your leg's up to full strength."

"The hell we will," he said with a playful growl, tackling her to the mattress. "I'll tell you what we're going to do." He paused for a dizzying kiss that made long-forgotten regions of her body hum. "Ever seen those bumper stickers around town? You know, the ones bull riders slap on their truck's rear windows?"

She reddened.

"I see you know the one?"

"Save a Horse, Ride a Cowboy?"

"That'd be the one. Well?"

"You want me to saddle up?"

"In a manner of speaking." He winked.

She blushed, then took them both for a wild ride.

"THIS IS COOL," Lindsay said as the hostess of Beefy's Steak House led them to their best table overlooking the small city park and fountain, high-lighted by the setting sun. "I've never been out for two dinners in one night, but Emily's mom just took us to Burger Barn."

"I'm glad you're having fun," Garret said, holding out a chair for the girl, then her mother.

"Why are we going out, though? I thought Mom was making meat loaf?"

"I, um, was," Connie said, clearing her throat. "But, Garret and I were fixing the roof and—"

The girl burst out laughing. "You? Fixed the roof?"

"What's funny about that?" Connie asked, giving her daughter's cute nose a tweak.

"Nothing," the girl said, hiding her giggle behind a menu.

"I think it's cool," Garret said. "You should've seen your mom up there. She was amazing."

"Why don't you quit your radio job and start roofing?" Lindsay suggested.

"Why would I want to do that?" When the girl didn't answer, but instead, fiddled with the paper wrapper of the straw the waitress had delivered along with three sweating glasses of water, Connie prodded, "Lindsay? Why would you ask such a thing? Especially when you know how much I love my show?"

"Mom, I'm sorry, but your show's getting

embarrassing. Ben's mom told him you and Garret are, like, *dating* on the radio."

"Would that be so awful?" Garret asked, closing his menu to focus on the girl.

"No, but…" The child wouldn't meet his gaze.

"But what, sweetie?" her mom coaxed.

Garret was emotionally unprepared for the evening's sudden nosedive.

"Mo-ommmm," Lindsay whined, gesturing with just her darting eyes that she wasn't about to divulge her true thoughts right there at the table in front of God and everyone but, most especially, him.

Clearing his throat, Garret took the hint, excusing himself to go to the restroom.

He did his business, washed his hands, then braced his hands on the brown tile counter, staring at himself in the mirror.

What was he doing?

Back in Virginia, he had a full life. Friends. An amazing career he'd worked damn hard for. Was he so hard up for a roll in the sack that he'd throw it all away? And sure, Lindsay was a sweet kid, but she wasn't *his* kid. She was Nathan's. For all Garret knew the girl's sudden change in attitude could be a sign that she was afraid Garret would replace her dad.

So many times, Garret had had this vision of him and Connie together again. He'd seen them having this big church wedding, maybe a year or so later, starting a family. Holding his tiny son or daughter in his arms for the first time would've been one of life's greatest joys. Bigger than earning his Trident, bigger than any mission he and his teams had ever completed.

One thing he'd never envisioned was stumbling across Connie like this. Finding her still as lovely as ever. Wanting her as badly as ever. He couldn't begin to process the fact that Connie might look the same, but inside, she was vastly different. She was a mother. A *mother*. And all that that implied. She had responsibilities he, who'd never even had a pet during his adult life, couldn't begin to comprehend.

He'd had no right to be with her that afternoon, just as he'd had no right to pretend for even an instant things weren't going to end badly between them for a second time.

After Monday's show, Constance unlocked her car's door, giving thanks to the man upstairs and his angels. In answer to her prayers, Garret— shock of all shocks—had been a perfect gentleman while discussing flower arranging and the meaning behind floral gifts, such as which shade of rose means hate, friendship or love and sharing listeners' favorite flower stories.

Garret had stayed behind in the office, saying

he had to make a few calls to friends and his CO. She'd offered to wait for him, but he'd waved her on, explaining that he had physical therapy that afternoon and wouldn't be able to hang with her and Lindsay that night, either, seeing how his mom needed her car.

Climbing into her Honda and cranking down the window to allow the day's pent-up heat an escape route, it occurred to her that everything about Garret's behavior had been off since Saturday night's dinner. On the surface, he'd been everything she and Lindsay could've hoped for in a dinner companion. Funny, thoughtful, attentive to their needs—even going so far as to recall her quirk of enjoying soy sauce with her steak, then asking the waitress to bring her a bottle.

She was halfway home before it occurred to her what the problem was. Garret had been *too* perfect. Too aware of pleasing her. Of using flawless table manners and keeping the conversation light and on a pleasant, never controversial, path.

For as long as she'd known him, part of what'd first drawn her to him was his zest for life. Though it maddened her that he never seemed overly concerned about life's pretenses, she respected how he'd followed a credo based upon what he'd perceived as right, rather than what anyone else had wanted. He never shied from a spirited debate, and now that she'd had a second to think about it, the evening had held plenty of opportunity for discourse.

In a nutshell, Garret hadn't really been Garret, but a shadow of the man she knew. He'd checked out on her, but why? Their precious afternoon had been start-to-finish perfection. So what went wrong? What'd spooked him?

At home, Constance puttered about the kitchen. She wiped countertops that were already clean. Finished up a book she'd long ago started. Lindsay came home, gave her a kiss and hug, grabbed a snack, then dashed off to care for and play with her rabbits.

And there Constance sat.

Alone.

Not so much different from the way she'd been before Garret had exploded back into her life, but yet indescribably different, seeing how she now recognized how all alone in the world she'd truly been. Yes, she'd had Lindsay, but the older Lindsay grew, the more independent she'd become. Constance's days and nights used to be consumed with caring for her. Helping her eat, dress and study. But now her daughter didn't need her as much, leaving Constance in the uncharted territory of having too much spare time on her hands.

Eyeing the phone, she made a split-second

decision to throw caution to the wind. Fingers crossed, already smiling, she dialed Garret's mother's. One ring sounded in her ear, then two and three until an answering machine picked up.

"Hi," said Garret's mom in a chirpy tone, *"you've reached Audrey Underwood. Please leave a message and I'll call you right back."*

Crestfallen to have apparently missed him, Constance hung up the phone.

"GARRET, HONEY?" his mom called from the living room.

Thank God, she'd been upstairs taking a shower. That way she wouldn't know that when the phone had rung and he'd seen Connie's name on the caller ID, he hadn't answered.

He couldn't say why, but he didn't have the energy to talk to her. Wanting her, and knowing it was morally wrong to have her, was exhausting.

He sat at the kitchen table, drowning his sorrows in a roast beef sandwich and milk.

Stepping up behind him, she asked, "Did you ever get a chance to unload those candles for me at the church?"

Oops. "I'll do it tomorrow, Mom."

"Don't forget," she said, marching into the kitchen to deliver her famous I'm-disappointed-in-you glare. "I brought them all home and transferred them to my trunk because Shirley was leaving for vacation. In this heat, they'll melt, and I'll get kicked off the decorating committee. I'd do it myself, but you always seem to be driving my car."

"Sorry. My mind's been on other things. If they're ruined, I'll buy you more."

"Honey, all I'm saying is—what's wrong? You look sick." She checked his forehead for fever. "You don't feel hot. Judging by the size of that sandwich, I'm guessing your stomach's fine. Things have been going great with Constance, right?"

From his seat at the kitchen table, he shrugged. "Something happened Saturday night. Guess it shook me up."

"What could possibly happen at Beefy's? It's Mule Shoe's finest."

Seeing the teasing sparkle in her eyes, he said, "Ha ha. I'm serious."

"I know," she said, patting his hand while refilling his iced tea. "Sorry. Go ahead."

He took a much-needed sip. "Okay, so we were sitting there, about to start in on what I thought would be a great night when Lindsay brought up the radio show, and how some friend's mother said Constance and I were dating. She said it with this horrible look on her face. Like she'd rather her mom hook up with an alien."

"Oh, honey," his mom said with a sympathetic

cluck. "Kids do that. Just blurt things without thinking."

"I know," he said. "And for the life of me, I can't figure out why I even care."

"Tell me if I'm overstepping, but my guess is that you care about Lindsay because you care about her mother."

"You're probably right. I felt a connection to the kid. Like we were pals. I just don't get what I must've done to make her turn on me like that."

"You did nothing—except maybe show you care for her mom a little too much. You have to remember, honey, Lindsay and Constance have been on their own for as long as that child can remember. She no doubt sees you as a potential threat."

"To what?"

"Getting between her and the most important person in her life."

Chapter Nine

"Your call was a nice surprise," Constance said to Garret the next morning, sliding into the back booth of Main Street Coffee Shop. "I tried calling you last night, but I guess you weren't home."

Not meeting her gaze, he said, "I went to bed early. Must not've heard the phone."

"That's okay."

"I didn't wake you, did I?" he asked. "Calling so early?"

She waved him off. "Are you kidding? I have to have Lindsay dressed and on her bus by seven-fifteen. I was just lingering over a second cup of tea." *Thinking of you.*

After a few minutes of small talk, the waitress brought Garret a coffee and Constance her third cup of orange pekoe.

They each ordered meals.

And then sat. Staring at each other like strangers.

Garret cleared his throat. "I can't stand this. One of us should say something."

"Okay…" Dread didn't begin to describe the knot in her stomach. This was it. She'd known better than to give herself wholly to him. Two days later and already, Navy Boy was giving her the old heave-ho.

Reaching across the table for her hands, he said, "I'm not even sure where to start."

"Dive right in," she said, trying to smile, knowing full well the gesture came nowhere near reaching her eyes.

"It's like this. I could be wrong here, but I was under the impression Lindsay and I were friends— if not well on our way to getting there. But when we were at dinner the other night, and Lindsay—"

"Is this about her pitching that little fit?"

"*Little* fit?" He shook his head before shooting her a look of disbelief over a sip of black coffee. "She glared at me like my head was crawling with lice—my *two* heads."

"Oh, she did not. You're making trouble where there's none."

"So you're saying she's tickled pink about us being together?"

Staring into her tea, she quietly asked, "Are we? Together?"

"Hell, I don't know." Shifting in the cramped

booth, he tried working the kinks out of his throbbing leg, but ended up kicking her. "Sorry."

"It's all right," she said. "I understand we're in uncharted territory."

"Uncharted?" He snorted. "More like off the known universe—at least mine."

Laughing, she gave his hands a squeeze. "After dinner, you know what she said after you'd excused yourself?"

"What?"

"Lindsay told me that she likes you a lot—very much considers you a friend—but if we're going to be an item, we need to be less vocal on air. Otherwise—and I'm reading between the lines here—we're a potential liability to her social standing by being embarrassing."

"That's it?"

She rolled her eyes. "You thought she'd told me to never see you again or that she was running away to Tulsa to dye her hair green, pierce her nose and get an I Hate Garret tattoo on her forehead?"

"The thought had crossed my mind."

"You're looking for problems where there are none." Look who's talking! If only Garret knew the real monster lurking just beyond his sight. That all of his confused feelings for Lindsay were grounded in shocking reality. So why, knowing that, was she now sitting here, trying to convince him to hang in there where the two of them were concerned? If she had an ounce of brains in her thick head, she'd agree with him that their relationship was detrimental to Lindsay. She'd file away their magical last time together under the heading: Good Times Best Forgotten.

She'd do all of that, that is, if she were smart. If she'd draw on the painful memories of her own past to once and for all realize a reunion with Garret could equal nothing but disaster for Lindsay and herself.

The waitress arrived with their meals.

A western omelet for Garret and scrambled eggs and toast for her. And though the conversation turned flirty and fun and the eggs were delicious and buttery, she couldn't get past feeling as if she were perched on the edge of a cliff.

Safety could be reached simply by backing up.

Or, she could jump.

"WELL, SON," Dr. Cy McCoy said Wednesday morning while scribbling on Garret's chart. His office hadn't changed a bit since Garret first met the man for a freshman sports physical in high school. The walls were still pale blue. Soft jazz still played from hidden speakers, giving away the man's after-hours love of music. Framed nighttime shots of his favorite cities still added life to what would've otherwise been a sterile room. Garret was proud to say he'd been to all of those cities—New York, San Francisco, Shanghai, Paris. "You're a lucky guy. From today's X-ray, your break has healed nicely and aside from a few lingering aches and pains, you're cleared to resume normal activity."

"Even my daily run?"

The doctor nodded. "Take it slow at first. No marathons your first day. But other than that, I want you to stick with your physical therapy a couple more weeks, then you're officially done."

"Just two weeks?"

"That should do it. Of course, if you feel any unusual pain, let me know, otherwise—" he held out his hand for Garret to shake "—don't wait another ten years before coming to see me."

Chuckling, Garret agreed.

After making small talk with the receptionist, Garret left the clinic not in the best of moods, which made no sense. When he'd first broken his leg, he'd been terrified of having it forever affect his career. He couldn't handle being tied to a desk. Worse yet, not being in the service at all.

But now? It sounded nuts even in his own head, but heading through muggy drizzle to his mom's car, it occurred to him that the reason he wasn't thrilled about finally receiving an all clear in regard to his health, was that it signaled the beginning of the end of his time in Mule Shoe.

While he should be happy about having an honorable out as far as she was concerned, Garret found himself not so much wanting an "out" but an "in."

But he was career Navy. In for life. Yes, guys got married and had kids all the time, but he wasn't anywhere near ready for such a step, was he? If not, what was he doing? Connie and her daughter deserved more than some guy playing house.

In the car, he cranked the engine, then flipped on the AC. Thunder rolled and mist turned to rain. The air smelled good. Mossy and clean.

Beyond his reunion with Connie, he'd enjoyed being back in the country. Having room for his spirit to roam. All this open space reminded him in subtle ways of being on the sea. Of having an unfettered horizon offering plenty of room to dream. Only problem was, considering how much dreaming of Connie he'd done of late, he'd probably had a little too much of a good thing.

Determined to get his thoughts on bringing his body and mind back to fighting condition, Garret flipped open his phone, placing a call to his CO. He'd been all ready to leave a message on the man's voice mail, but was caught off guard when his secretary patched him through.

"Underwood. Good hearing from you. How's the family?"

Connie and Lindsay? They're great, sir. Never looked better. You should see my girl wrangle her pet rabbits. Cute as a button—the bunnies and the girl. And Connie? She's gorgeous as ever. She'll blow everyone away in her new dress for the Fourth of July Firecracker Ball.

"Mom's great, sir. Thanks for asking."

"And the leg?"

"That's the reason I'm calling. Aside from a couple more weeks PT, my doc just gave me the all clear."

"Great. That's what I've been hoping to hear."

"Thank you, sir."

"All right, now that you're back in working order, I'll have your base doc e-mail you a workout schedule. Graded. Similar to your BUD/S training, but somewhat accelerated. Still, I don't want you falling victim to a stress fracture at this stage of the game."

Garret inwardly moaned. "Yes, sir."

"In the meantime, unless something pressing comes up, I want you focused on regaining your physical strength."

"Yes, sir."

"Call two weeks from today to apprise me of your status."

"Yes, sir."

"Oh, and Underwood?"

"Yes?"

"Hooyah."

"Hooyah, sir." *Hooyah.* When Garret flipped shut his phone, it was with a renewed sense of mourning.

Far from celebrating his pending return to normal life, it was as if he'd only just now begun *normal* life and everything prior had been a dream. He was no longer a SEAL, but a mixed-up high-school kid, heading off to basic training, alternately hating and missing his girl.

So far, she hadn't shared squat with him as to why she'd dumped him for Nathan. Maybe he'd never really know. Truth of the matter was, the more he was with her, the less he cared and the more he felt one hundred percent focused on nothing but letting bygones be bygones, then picking up where they'd left off.

"YOU SERIOUSLY SHOULDN'T be doing this," Connie said on a gloomy, but hot, Saturday morning while Garret stood on a ladder, paint scraper in hand. "In fact, if your mother found out about this, I'm pretty sure she'd ground you for life."

He laughed. "Then it's a good thing she doesn't

know half of what I do for a living. Besides which, I told you, the doctor said I'm fine, and my CO said to get off the couch and onto my—"

"Geez, Garret," Lindsay said, wandering out the front porch door, tilting her head back to assess his morning's progress. Nose wrinkled, she said, "You're not going very fast."

"Thanks," he said. "Like to see you try."

"Okay." Hands on her hips, chin raised in a stubborn pose reminding him of her mother's obstinate streak, she asked, "Got another one of those?"

"A scraper?"

"Uh-huh."

"Sure, I've got another. Wanna race?" He glanced Connie's way to find her grinning, but shaking her head. "What's your problem?"

"Only that I have two big kids on my hands. What am I going to do with you?"

Lindsay was already at the foot of the porch stairs, rummaging through Garret's tool bucket. "You can referee, Mom."

"Yeah, *Mom*." Garret shot Connie a wink. As usual, she looked cute this morning, but in a non-business way. She always looked great in her uptight work suits and prim dresses, but he much preferred her current choice of faded jean cutoffs and a ratty blue Mule Shoe Miners T-shirt that hugged her tempting curves. "You be the judge of who wins."

"Okay, but under one condition."

"What's that?" Garret asked.

Hands on her hips, looking very much like her daughter, she said, "You both have to compete while on the ground. We'll measure off same-sized siding patches and let the games begin—only I want in on the action, too."

Lindsay groaned, but best as Garret could tell, it was a good-natured lament.

Ten minutes later, after establishing an intricate set of rules and Lindsay running inside to unearth a stopwatch from her closet floor, the girl counted them down. "Okay, everyone start in three, two, one—wait." Glancing at both grown-ups, she scrunched her face and asked, "What's the prize?"

"Good question," Garret said, glancing at Connie. "Any ideas?"

"I don't have money to buy anything," Lindsay said.

"Honey, it doesn't have to be store bought," Connie pointed out. "The losers could bake cookies for the winner. Maybe be their servant for the day."

"Really?" Lindsay's eyes widened. "That'd be cool, bossing you guys around."

"Hey," Garret protested, "when I win, that'll be the other way around."

"What about when *I* win?" Connie asked,

giving him a laughing jab, then turning her tickling fingers on Lindsay.

After more taunting and wrestling and giggling, Lindsay counted them off again. "Three, two, one—go!"

Garret started off strong with his usual urge to win, but lost focus when he glanced at Lindsay.

She gave the task her all, arms pumping to make peeling paint fly. She'd tucked her lower lip into her mouth and her forehead was furrowed in concentration. Her outfit of pink sweatpants and a matching pink T-shirt were dirt smudged, but he was impressed with her determination. So impressed, he found himself in the unheard of territory of wanting to lose so that she could win.

Poor Connie never had a chance.

"What's the matter?" he teased. "Not want to get those fancy nails dirty?"

"I worked a long time on these," she said, wagging sexy red tips at him.

"I'd have greater appreciation for your efforts," he said low enough for only her to hear, "if you'd run those up my bare chest."

"Hush," she said, cheeks more colorful than her nails.

"'Course, you could run 'em over other spots, too. Say, at an exotic locale like Owen Cate's boathouse. I saw him the other day. Asked where he hides his key."

"Stop," she said, still blushing to glance Lindsay's way only to find the girl working harder than ever. "You're awful."

"True, but judging by that smile of yours, you still get the occasional hankering to get busy in unconventional places."

Lindsay's timer went off.

"Oh," Connie complained to Garret. "You so cheated by—"

"What did he do, Mom?" Lindsay asked. "Should he be disqualified?"

"Wouldn't matter anyway," he said with a rogue's wink to her mother, "seeing how, from the looks of your section, you won."

"Really?" Lindsay's smile widened while surveying her competition's work—or lack thereof. "I did win. *Yes!* You're both my servants and my first command is for you to make me blueberry pancakes."

"Whoa," Garret said, surveying the darkening sky, "shouldn't I get back to scraping in case it rains?"

Connie teased, "Don't even think about weaseling out of this, mister. You lost, too. Fair and square."

"All right," he said, hooking his arms around Connie's shoulders after they'd put up their tools and headed in the house. Lindsay had run ahead, and from the *zinging, zoinking* and *boinking* sounds floating through the open living room windows, she was parked on the sofa, watching cartoons. "I'll be a willing servant for the day, but don't think I'm giving up on that boathouse trip."

Elbowing his ribs, she said, "You're awful."

"I fully agree, but I don't hear you protesting the trip. That mean you're looking forward to it, too?"

His question earned another jab.

"HERE YOU GO, your highness," Constance overheard Garret croon from the living room where her daughter had set up her throne. He was delivering her latest snack order—a grilled cheese sandwich and chocolate milk shake. Constance had been all for telling Lindsay to take it easy on her list of demands, but he'd asked her to let the kid go on a while longer.

Overall, right down to the much-needed rain hammering the windows, it'd been an outrageously perfect day. Now that Garret and Lindsay were getting along better, during a marathon Trivial Pursuit game—also at Lindsay's request—the three of them had begun to feel like a family.

Only that wasn't necessarily a good thing. When her daughter was around, Connie and Garret had decided to pretend to be just friends. Trouble was, every time she was alone with him, Garret would whisper sexy innuendos, which only resulted in more frustration.

Of course, Constance wanted to be with him again in an intimate way, but she couldn't see any possibility of accomplishing that without ultimately getting hurt.

Which brought up another nagging issue—Lindsay's paternity. Every time Constance saw Lindsay and Garret together, getting on so well, she'd get this insane urge to tell him—both of them—*everything*.

The phone rang once. Lindsay must've gotten it.

Good, seeing how Constance was hardly in the right frame of mind for small talk.

"What's got you so deep in thought?" Garret asked a few minutes later, setting Lindsay's serving tray on the counter, then hopping up behind her to ease his hands around her waist. Hot breath in her ear, he whispered, "Smile. I have it on good authority a certain someone just got invited for a sleepover at her friend Mindy's."

"Hmm…interesting."

"*Just* interesting?" He nuzzled her neck and growled. While she wanted to hold tight to her fear of what her attraction to him might bring, with his maddeningly playful behaviour, her resolve didn't stand a chance.

"All right, maybe a little more in the realm of exhilarating, but I can't very well let you know that, can I?"

"Why not?" he asked, kissing her throat. From the living room, Constance heard her daughter giggle, telling her that Lindsay was still on the phone.

Taking a ridiculous leap of faith, she cupped his cheeks, raising those roving lips of his to hers. After soundly kissing him, she whispered, "I can't tell you such things because I shouldn't even like you, let alone think of mostly nothing but you 24/7."

He kissed her right back. "Seeing how I'm in the same boat, I say go with it."

"What happens when you leave?" she dared ask, heart pounding. *What if you learn the truth about Lindsay?*

"We're not going to think about it till it's time." He kissed her deeper and harder, igniting a hunger in her soul.

Breasts aching, lower regions brushing against Garret's hardness, the miniscule part of her that spent every waking moment being responsible asked, "Is that wise?"

"At the moment," he said, voice husky, eyes half-closed, "I don't much give a damn."

"Geez, guys," Lindsay said, strolling into the kitchen to hang up the cordless phone. "Could you get a room?"

"Lindsay!" Constance said, shocked not just to be caught by her daughter, but to hear that sort of worldly phrase pass her lips. "Where'd you learn that expression?"

"The fifth graders. But why're you mad at me? You're the one kissing in the middle of the kitchen."

Garret groaned. Here we go again. "Look, kiddo—"

"I'm not a kid," she said, chin raised, "but a young lady."

"Sorry," he said, "my mistake. What wasn't a mistake is me being affectionate with your mother. I like her, Lindsay—a lot."

"Oh."

Connie pressed her hands to his chest, "Garret, you don't have to—"

"Yes, dammit—pardon my French—I do."

"It's okay," Lindsay said. "Your French. The fifth graders say that all the time, too."

"What kind of school am I sending you to?" Connie asked with a moan.

"A normal school," Garret said. "You, Miz History Lover, are the only one who walks around in an eighteenth-century-manners bubble. The rest of us reside in reality."

"Yeah, Mom."

Rubbing her forehead, Connie mumbled, "This isn't happening."

"Yes, it is," he said, dragging her around to face him. "Lindsay and I are performing a manners intervention—"

Lindsay giggled.

"Right now," Garret continued, "say something completely inappropriate. Come on, I know it's hard, but it's for your own good."

"Come on, Mom. You can do it."

"You two have lost your minds. And how did it happen that all of a sudden I'm being ganged up on?" Leaving him, Connie took a mug from the cabinet, set it on the counter, then filled the teakettle with water before setting it on the stove and turning on the flame.

"Please, Mom, you have always been kind of uptight—especially lately—at least when Garret's not here."

Interesting, Garret thought, content to let this surprise flare-up between his beauties run its course.

"How can you say that, when I've been serving you all day? Letting you get away with pretty much any stunt you've pulled?"

"That's just today. What about before Garret even got here? How I catch you frowning, but then you smile and tell me everything's fine. I'm not dumb, Mom. I know when you're faking being happy."

Connie had been facing the stove, but now, arms tightly crossed, she turned to glare at her daughter.

"Well?" Garret cleared his throat. "As an impartial observer here, Lindsay, I've gotta know, just now, when you walked in on us and caught your uptight mother kissing, did she look real happy or faking-it happy?"

The girl said, "She was for real happy."

"What?" Garret asked, mostly for Connie's benefit, seeing how his hearing was a hundred percent. "Could you please repeat that?"

The kid—pardon, young woman—grinned. "Mom looked *really* happy kissing you—even happier than when the plumber told her the sink thingee was just clogged and wouldn't cost much to fix."

"Lindsay, hush," Connie said.

"I don't want to hush. I worry about you, but there's no one to talk to but my friends or Daddy, but then he starts looking or sounding worried, so most times I don't talk to him about it, either."

"When did you last call your, um, father?" Connie asked.

"Yesterday. He was nice, but sounded grumpy."

"He was probably super busy with work," Connie said.

"You always say that. I think he just doesn't love me. This is the worst day ever!" And with that, she tore out of the kitchen and up the stairs fast enough to rattle the decorator plates hanging from the kitchen wall.

"Good grief," Connie said, sitting at the kitchen table. "What brought on all of that? And when did my little girl become so adept at reading my feelings?"

Easing behind her for a hug, Garret asked, "The issue worrying me is why have you been so unhappy?"

"I'm not. Really."

Spinning her to face him, seeing right off she was lying just by the lack of light in her eyes, he said, "It's me you're talking to. Let's hear it."

"I don't know," she said with a shrug. "Who's to say what happiness even is? I have a wonderful life. A healthy, beautiful daughter who gets great grades and didn't use to sass too much. I've been blessed with a great job I may even get to keep since you climbed aboard—thanks." She paused to gift him with a quick kiss. "Everything's great. I'm lucky."

"But there's still something bothering you and it concerns me."

"Well, it shouldn't."

"Why not? I…" What? Was he about to say he loved her? But did he? He certainly had once, but hadn't he already established that he wouldn't put himself through that kind of stress again? She'd dumped him—hard. By her daughter's admission, and now her own, she was admittedly having a tough time. If anything, shouldn't that have him running to his mom's as fast as his newly healed leg could carry him?

So why did he suddenly want nothing more than to put a smile on Connie's face? And not just temporarily, but for the rest of her life?

"Garret?" she asked, searching his features. "What were you about to say?"

I love you. I'm dangerously close to loving your kid. I want to take care of you and give you days filled with laughter and nights spent in each other's arms.

He wanted to say all of that, but couldn't. Why? Because his head knew loving Connie could lead to disaster, but his heart didn't care?

"Garret?" she asked, hand on his shoulder. "You okay?"

"Sure," he said with what was probably too broad a smile. "I'm great."

"Promise?"

"Hell, yeah," he said, planting a kiss on her forehead. "And hey, once we drop Lindsay off at Mindy's, wanna go grab a couple steaks at Beefy's?"

"Sure. Let me see if she's calmed down enough to go."

Swell. And while you do that, I'll convince myself I'm not a fool for wanting to make love with you for the rest of my life.

Chapter Ten

"Where are we?" Constance asked, peering beyond the windows of Garret's mom's Caddie into inky darkness.

"You don't know?" His smile was only visible with help from the dash lights' glow.

Patting her overly full stomach, she said, "With a half side of beef in me, it's a wonder I even know my own name."

"I'm hurt."

"That I ate so much?"

"Heh, heh, heh." While she grinned, he pulled the car onto a dirt road that looked more like a trail. Dusty weeds grew along the shoulders and up the center. "I'm hurt you don't recognize this place."

Leaning forward, bracing her hands on the dash, she said, "Give me a minute, I'm working through the sour-cream-and-butter haze left by the loaded baked potato."

"Take your time—but not too much. If you haven't guessed before we get there, I'm turning this tank around and putting you straight to bed—alone."

"Ouch. How am I supposed to concentrate with that kind of threat hanging over my head?"

"Oh, please. Like I can concentrate with you shoved into that crime scene of a dress?"

"What's that supposed to mean? I love this dress—not that I get to wear it all that much." The low-cut, scarlet confection she'd splurged on for their five-year high school reunion in the secret hope Garret would be there, was hardly something you threw on for a quick trip to the store. Still, it felt good knowing that even after all this time, it'd finally been seen by the only eyes that mattered.

"Good. I'd have to chase you around, tossing napkins over all that cleavage."

"There's not that much," she said, gazing down.

"The hell there isn't. Did you see how Bud Harris eyed you? For a while there, thought I might have to take him out for a rumble."

"Jealous?" *I hope.*

He growled, then slowed to make another turn onto an even sorrier excuse for a road.

Dark as it was, she'd truly been clueless about where he could be heading, but as he brought the car to the crest of a hill, pausing for her to drink in the panoramic view, her breath caught in her throat.

Moonlight played on Lake Mule Shoe's waves, transforming what by day was a pretty lake into a glistening diamond field.

Making the sight even more memorable was the way Garret had tugged her over to join him after turning off the car and unfastening his seat belt. "Well? Figure it out?"

"We're on our way to Owen's boathouse. I can't believe I didn't recognize it earlier."

He placed a hasty kiss to the crown of her head. "Well, seeing how I'm still high from eating both of our bowls of ice cream for dessert, guess I'll let it slide."

"Gee, thanks." She snuggled closer. "Mmm…I'd forgotten how good it feels being held."

"By me? Or just any guy who strolls along?"

"Seriously, I've been on a couple so-so blind dates and setups thoughtfully arranged by my friends, but—and this should be good for your ego—there's never been anyone like you."

Leaning his head against hers, he sighed.

"Okay, what does that mean?"

"All I was trying to say is ditto." He gave her a squeeze. "Lord knows I've tried replacing you. Blondes and redheads. Studious beauties with glasses."

"You've *been* with all those women?" Scooting away from him so she could face him, she said,

"Good grief, Garret. I just went on dates, but it sounds like you—"

He kissed her hard, fast and claiming. "I said I tried dating other women. That doesn't mean I was with all of them. Sad fact is that you're apparently like some mysterious jungle fever. Once you entered my bloodstream, I've not been able to get you out." Tracing her jaw with such tenderness she wanted to weep from the joy of not just his touch but his words, he said, "Sometimes I almost felt free of you, but then the fever went and reared its disconcerting head."

"Did—" she licked her lips "—did you want to be free of me?"

"Truthfully? Heck, yeah. We don't mix. Talk about polar opposites in every regard. But then there's that one undefinable something that even after all these years, keeps pulling us back."

"I know what you mean."

"So?" he teased, nuzzling her earlobe with warm, ice-cream-scented breath, "ready to take the next step in reinforcing our misery?"

"Hurry up, Garret!" Constance shouted a few minutes later, shivering outside Owen's boathouse. "It's chilly out here. And what're you doing that's taking so long?"

"Have you always been this demanding?" called a muffled voice from inside.

"Sorry! But it's not everyday I'm blindfolded and then abandoned on a rickety bench in the middle of nowhere!"

"You'll survive."

Constance grinned and shook her head.

The silky scarf Garret had covered her eyes with smelled faintly of his yummy, citrus-based after-shave, which only made this brief separation that much tougher.

The night came alive around her with more scents of musky, fishy water and the honeysuckle kissing the boathouse's south wall.

Humming cicadas battled chirping crickets for who could make the most noise. The plunk of waves against Owen's bass boat reminded Constance of long-ago fishing trips where she and Garret caught more of each other than the crappie they'd set out to snag. Those were such amazing times. Was she being foolish to think for one minute the two of them could ever find what they'd lost—or rather, what she'd thrown away by having lied to him in the first place?

More and more since Garret had been back, she'd wanted to tell him about his daughter, but fear of losing what they'd found once more held that confession at bay.

A far-off coyote's lonely call made her shiver.

"Garret? Are you hurrying?" she teased, trying

to find her once playful mood. "There're man-eaters out here!"

"Give me a break! I'm going as fast as I can with one good leg!"

Laughing, she called, "Oh sure, pull out the old one good leg excuse!"

Everything would be all right. Garret was a kind, wonderful man. Sure, when he found out about Lindsay, he'd be understandably upset, but he'd ultimately forgive her, right?

Whoa. When had she even made the decision to tell him? Was she kidding herself by thinking Garret would hear he was a father and they'd all live happily every after?

"Okay, gorgeous! Prepare to be dazzled!"

"Does that mean I can take my blindfold off?"

"Sorry, princess, but that's my job! You just sit tight."

Sit tight. That's just what she intended to do. Steal this one more precious moment, then tell him later. *Much* later.

"OH, GARRET…it's amazing. But where'd you get the candles?"

"I have my sources," he said, sending up a silent prayer that he could replenish them before his mom discovered them missing. There'd be hell to pay if he didn't, but to see Connie's smile, it was worth it.

"Well, wherever you got them, I'm highly impressed—and touched—that you'd go to all this trouble for me. It's beautiful."

Yeah, if he said so himself, the dusty old place did look pretty damned good.

"You're the beautiful one," he said, pulling her into his arms. "When holding you feels so good, remind me again why we broke up?"

The minute the question was out, he regretted it, seeing how the ugly answer now hung between them and he'd wanted to make this night extra special. What he regretted even more were the instant tears glistening in Connie's big blue eyes.

"Sorry," he said while she looked up at him with an unreadable expression. Pain? Fear? Confusion?

"No." She sniffled. "We both know good and well everything bad between us is because of me."

He tried grasping her hand, but for once she'd tugged harder than he had and he let her get away. Just as he had all those years ago. Sure he could've stuck around and fought for her, but he'd figured what was the point if she didn't want him. Why give up his dreams if all she desired was another guy? "Tell me something," he said with her clear across the cathedral-like space, candlelight reflecting off the green, glassy water.

"What?"

"Since we're on the subject, back when I caught

you and Nathan making out at John Dugger's party, and you told me Nathan was the guy you truly wanted, how come you didn't fight harder to keep your marriage alive?"

"Do we have to rehash ancient history?" She'd lowered herself onto one of the low-riding pair of beach chairs he'd set up on the wood-planked floor. Between them was a chilled bottle of champagne he'd secretly bought from Beefy's night manager.

He'd have joined her, but at the last minute, fearing a collision of his still-stiff leg and the rough wood planks, he made a strategic decision to remain standing. Besides, this was one question he didn't want Connie weaseling out of. "How's it ancient history if the answer's relevant to what we're now going through?"

"I thought we were here for… You know?" She reddened. Popping the cork on the champagne, once it'd stopped foaming, she held it to her entirely too kissable lips for a good, long swig.

"Trust me…" he said, already hard at the mere mention of what Connie implied, "we'll get to *that* shortly, but for now, tell me, if you supposedly loved Nathan so much that it drove you away from me and straight into his arms, why didn't it last? Why aren't you still with him? You'd for damn sure be living a better life. You'd be queen of the whole county. Reigning supreme over country-club dances and all that other high falutin' BS you claim to be so fond of."

"Language!"

"For the last time," he said between ground teeth, thumping his hand against the nearest support column in frustration over his leg still hurting when he bent it to look her square in her eyes. "Be straight with me."

"It's none of your business."

"None of my business?" He nearly choked on his bitter laugh. "What you did nearly destroyed me to the point that, ten years later, I'm still not over you. I'd say that very much makes it my business."

"It doesn't matter, okay? Please, just leave it alone."

"Why?"

"B-because you've gone to such trouble to make this messy old place magical, and—" She swiped at the couple tears marring her cheeks.

"And what?"

"And because I was already pregnant when you saw us, okay? There? Are you happy? Is that what you wanted to hear?"

Hands to his forehead, soul reeling, he felt eighteen again, consumed by jealous rage. "You slept with that fool? Even before I caught you kissing?"

She didn't say a word. Just sat there with that damned unreadable mask on her face.

"I'll take that as a yes, otherwise Lindsay would have to be mine, and even you wouldn't be so cruel as to keep my own child from me all these years?"

Still she was silent.

"Connie, tell me you wouldn't have done that, or so help me, I'm not sure what I'll do."

She barely shook her head.

He paced. "So? Go on? If you supposedly loved Nathan enough to sleep with him while you were still with me, why didn't you stay together? Can't you see I'm dying here to know?"

She stood, ran to him, throwing herself against him so hard, he nearly toppled from the force.

"I'm sorry," she said, raining a hundred tiny kisses over his chest and throat and finally, his face. "I'm so sorry. Please, Garret. Please believe me when I tell you you're the only man I've ever loved." By now, she was hysterically sobbing and he grabbed hold of her wrists to stop her from painfully kneading his chest.

"Stop!" he ordered, only she wasn't some raw recruit, but the woman he now knew, for better or worse, beyond a shadow of any doubt, he loved. He'd always loved her, never—no matter how hard he'd tried—been able to stop. "Shh…" he muttered, releasing her wrists to pull her limp body into his arms. "Please stop crying." Over and over, he smoothed her hair, her back, anything to stop her tears. The depth of her emotion told him she was truly sorry, but it still hadn't told him why she'd turned away from him to be with his best friend.

Violently shaking her head, she said, "Losing you hurts too bad."

"I'm not going anywhere. I never would've gone anywhere. Remember? You're the one who threw me away. After my training, I would've come back, but you never gave me a chance."

"No." She pulled back. "No, that's where you're wrong. I loved you so much, I didn't throw you away, I pushed you away."

"What?" He scratched his head. This night was growing more bizarre by the second.

"All your life, you'd wanted to join the Navy. Become a big, tough SEAL. It's all you ever talked about. You were consumed. It was your dream. And I knew all about dreams, seeing how back then, I still had them."

"You still could," he said.

She again shook her head. "It's too late for me. But you got yours—because I let you."

"You *let* me?" He snorted. "That's the biggest pile of horse crap I've ever—"

"Belittle me if you want, Garret, but it's true. I knew you'd never leave me, and then you'd have been stuck in this town forever. You were too good for that, so I pretended to be madly in love with

Nathan and, you have to admit, it worked. You left for basic training and voilà…a SEAL was born. But then I got pregnant and everything changed. We had to get married."

"So you're saying every single bit of what went down between you and Nathan was a carefully calculated lie? My supposed best friend was in on it, too?"

"At the time, I didn't want to think it was a lie. I—I told myself he was a great guy. Over time, we'd make it work. He agreed to that b-because of the baby, our getting married was for the best."

"Wait a minute… What about you telling me you'd never slept with him until after we broke up?"

"Oh my God, Garret, can you please just give it a rest? Maybe there's more of your father in you than you'd like to admit."

"What's that supposed to mean?"

"Just that maybe you'd have made a good attorney after all. Maybe if I hadn't tried to manipulate your future, you'd have had a perfectly good life…."

"Here? With you? And Lindsay would be my kid instead of Nathan's? Do you know how many times I've played that scenario out in my head? Why, Connie? Even after you found out you were carrying Nathan's child, why didn't you come to me? We could've worked something out. We could've gotten married."

"Oh, please. Do you honestly think you could've made it through your training with a pregnant wife tagging along?"

"I damn sure would've liked the opportunity to have tried."

Snatching the champagne bottle, she raised it high, "Well here's to the glory of hindsight." She took three quick swigs, then said, "Take me home. Then I want you to go out and find a woman who actually deserves you."

"I thought I already had," he said softly.

She laughed before taking another drink. "Yeah, well, you thought wrong. If you haven't figured it out by now, I'm an awful person."

"Give me that bottle," he said.

"No." She tucked it between her breasts.

"You never have been able to hold your liquor."

"Or my man."

He rolled his eyes.

"I am sorry, Garret."

"I know. Me, too."

"So where does that leave us?" She hiccupped. He wished the evening had turned out differently, but the spell was broken.

He wasn't sure what to think. About her, him, his job. He wasn't sure what to think about anything, really. Other than that since losing Connie the first time, never had he felt quite so bone-weary tired.

Chapter Eleven

"You look like hell," Audrey said without fanfare Sunday morning, refilling Garret's mug. He sat at the kitchen table, staring out at the cattle, recalling days when the only thing on his mind had been downing a bowl of Cap'n Crunch, feeding the herd, then running off with his friends to explore in the woods. "Want to go with me to church? Might do you good."

He laughed.

"So what happened now between you and Constance? Don't tell me you had another fight?"

Sipping his coffee, he said, "Let's just say it was quite a night—only not the way I'd planned."

"Sorry," she said, pressing a kiss to his forehead before heading off to fix her daily bowl of Grape-Nuts, leaving him with the scent of the same floral perfume she'd worn since the dawn of time.

"You ever think of finding a new perfume?"

"No. Why?" She poured her cereal into a bowl.

"No reason, just thought you might get tired of it, and I'd find you something new."

Joining him at the table, she said, "I don't get tired of things I love. Speaking of things we love, when will you give up this cat-and-mouse game with Constance and officially forgive the poor girl? I'd say her years of playing spinster have been more than enough restitution for her sins."

"What then? I live in Virginia and travel constantly. Where could a relationship between us possibly go?"

"I'm not saying you should rush into anything, but there are married folks in the Navy. When I first met your father, he was on leave from 'Nam. You don't think that was a tough separation?"

"I know, it's just that—"

"Sweetheart, I'm not saying Constance didn't put you through an emotional wringer. When you left for basic training, knowing she'd taken up with Nathan, it was all I could do not to claw her eyes out every time we met. But now…" She shrugged. "I almost feel sorry for the girl."

"Sorry enough to offer up your only son?" He cocked an eyebrow.

Grin tugging the corners of her lips, she patted his hand. "All I'm doing is offering up a shot at hope—for both of you. Honey, I'm your mother.

Worrying is my job. The fact that after all this time, when you two get together your chemistry is like lightning in a jar, speaks volumes."

He laughed. "On what?"

"That maybe it's time both of you got a second chance."

THAT AFTERNOON, GARRET thought about his mother's words. He couldn't believe the spark between Connie and him was strong enough for even his mother to see. What did it mean? Was it significant that things physically between them were still great? That he still loved to talk with Connie and felt all at once calmed and happy by her smile? Was all of that enough to forget everything they'd been through? On the flip side, what if he gave up on them now? Would he spend the rest of his life kicking himself for never having found out?

The question was one he pondered the entire day.

He thought about it while hiking through the woods, the ghost of the boy and teen he'd once been tagging along, urging him to return to his roots. The man he was now sent mixed messages. What Connie had done had hurt him deeply, but he'd come full circle to realize, above anything else in his life, she mattered most. His love for her had never died, only become a slow burn he'd tried to extinguish, but had never quite succeeded. Constance Price was a part of him. For better or for worse, he couldn't—wouldn't—ever let her go again.

ON AIR MONDAY, Constance took a deep breath, scooted an inch farther from Garret, whose presence crowded the room, then said into the microphone in what she hoped was her serene voice, "Thank you, Kay, for your insightful additions to our lively discussion of appropriate retirement gifts for coworkers, family and friends. Along this same line, we'd love to hear your favorite retirement stories—either personal or that of a coworker or friend. How did your own, or their retirement make you feel? Overjoyed? Put out to pasture? Let us know. Renee-Marie, do you have our next caller?"

"I sure do, Miss Manners. Marsha, from Osage, has a question for you regarding her father's upcoming retirement party."

"Thank you, Renee-Marie," Constance said, praying the next fifteen minutes would go by faster than the earlier portions of the show. "Marsha, how can we help?"

"First off," Marsha said, *"I want you to know how much I highly respect your opinion, Miss Manners. You're everything I aspire to be."*

"Well, thank you," she said, warmed that at least someone thought she was fit to remain on the planet.

Garret snorted.

Ignoring him, she asked the caller, "How can I help with your father's big day?"

"Well, my two older brothers insist on decorating the Saint James Parish hall where Daddy's reception is being held with black balloons, but I say that would be not only disrespectful to Daddy, but to our Heavenly Father, as well."

"Marsha, I couldn't agree more. You hold tight to your convictions on this and encourage your brothers to reconsider going with a festive theme of silver or gold. Or, if you're a true adventuress, perhaps use both for a really special touch."

"Oh, that does sound lovely," the caller said. *"Thank you so very much."*

"You are so very welcome."

"Okay," her cohost said, leaning forward in his chair, in the process, brushing her forearm in the most maddening way. "Can I just say this topic is so incredibly boring crickets are chirping in my ears?"

"You may say it," Constance said, "but judging by the relieved tone in our last caller's voice, you'd be very wrong. Renee-Marie, do you have our next caller?"

"I sure do, and this one'll be a treat. We have Audrey on line six."

A treat? Constance's stomach sank.

"Garret, honey, this is your mother, and I have to say that at the moment, I'm madder than a wet hornet at you."

Squeezing her eyes shut tight, Constance silently groaned. This was indeed bad. What had happened to her once peaceful, predictable show?

"Hey, Mom. I'm kinda busy here, but what'd I do this time?"

"First, there's that matter we discussed yesterday morning that I'm gathering you still haven't had the fortitude to tackle—"

"Mom, with all due respect, please stay out of it."

"I will, and am, but one issue I'm not staying out of is getting to the bottom of what happened to my candles. My friend, Shirley, picked me up this morning so we could replace the altar candles, and I headed to the storeroom to replenish the stock. Imagine my everlasting surprise, when I discovered the two hundred dollars worth of candles I'd purchased with church funds weren't there. Have you left them in my trunk all this time? And if so, they're probably a melted, goopy mess all over my new car's carpet."

"They're not in the trunk, Mom."

"How do you know? In between all this gallivanting you've been doing in my pride and joy, you've had time to check the trunk?"

"Mrs. Underwood…" Constance cleared her

throat. Yes, she should stay quiet, but something deep inside leaped to Garret's defense. "This is a tad off topic, but he knows where the candles are, because he, um, used them to woo me." To admit such a thing publicly when, for a decade, she'd been such a private person had Constance's cheeks flaming. Still, she felt oddly glad about the confession. About being able to help Garret—even with something so silly.

The phone lines glowed a solid wall of red.

Felix burst into Renee-Marie's booth to flash a thumbs-up sign through the soundproof window.

"Woo you?" Audrey asked. *"But then, Garret, honey, after that, did you—"* she cleared her throat *"—you know, do what we talked about?"*

"Mom, I love you dearly, but has anyone ever told you you have a big mouth?"

He pressed the disconnect button, then asked Renee-Marie, "Do we have another caller?"

The producer grinned. "Only about two thousand."

AFTER WORK, ALONE in the rambling farmhouse she'd lived in her entire life, Constance scrubbed the laminate counter with everything in her, but couldn't seem to get it clean.

Sure it's the counter you need cleansed, or your guilty conscience?

She kept scrubbing.

Her conscience was fine. Sort of. She'd let most of what'd been eating her out of the proverbial bag Saturday night. Everything except the biggest bomb of all.

She stopped scrubbing to lean her elbows on the counter and sigh. The traces of moisture left from the wet rag soaked into her pea green sweatshirt, but she didn't care—about anything. All she used to think so vital to her happiness— getting the house painted, replacing her car's air conditioner, having enough cash left at the end of the week to buy bunny food—none of it mattered anymore, because until Garret had returned, though it'd taken her ten-year-old daughter to ultimately point it out, Constance had only been playacting at life. Going through the motions.

In the studio earlier that afternoon, his nearness had been maddening, but at the same time invigorating. Because she was alone now with no one but herself to hear, she could admit that without him, life was gray with a few dazzling glimpses of color provided by her little girl.

His little girl.

She'd been close to telling him the whole truth, but then he'd gotten so angry over the very thought of her having lied all this time, she couldn't. So where did that leave her? She couldn't go forward or backward. She was stuck in this god-awful purgatory with no hope for escape.

The back door creaked open.

Constance looked that way, expecting Lindsay, but it was Garret, backlit by brilliant afternoon sun. Had he always been so big? Imposing? Achingly handsome?

"Hey," he said before shutting the door.

"Hey."

"You ran out of the studio so fast we didn't have time to talk."

She sighed, backing up to the counter to heft herself onto it. "Come on, what's really left to say?"

"That's seriously how you feel? Or are you in self-protection mode?"

"What's that mean?"

"You made some pretty incriminating confessions the other night. So now are you just planning on sitting here, hating yourself? Or me? Or Nathan?"

"If you're here to make me feel worse, sorry, I'm pretty much bottomed out."

"Christ, Connie…" He strolled across the kitchen, easing between her legs. Hands cupping her cheeks, he kissed her, slowly, tenderly, with all the love and care she didn't deserve. "Haven't you figured it out? I love you. I never stopped loving you."

"But—"

He kissed away her every objection.

The back door creaked open. *"Ew,"* Lindsay said. "You two kissing again?"

Leaving her to turn his back to the counter, Garret said, "Nice to see you, too, squirt."

"Hey, if I'm a squirt, then you're a giant."

"Ugh," Garret said with a big, goofy smile. Faking a mortal wound by the girl's sharp tongue, he clutched his chest. "You got me."

"Yes." Apparently used to them kissing, and to joking around with ever-present Garret, Lindsay ignored both adults to focus on the contents of the fridge.

"Linds?" Garret asked.

"Yeah?" She poked her head out from the open fridge door.

"Think we could talk for a sec?"

She glanced at her mom, then back at him. "I guess. What's up?"

"Nothing much," he said. "At least not yet. Come on." Leading her to the front porch, he called out for Connie to hang tight.

"Everything okay?" Lindsay asked. "Mom's been acting funny ever since I got home from Mindy's Sunday morning."

He eased onto the porch's top step. "Close the door and come have a seat. I'll explain."

"'Kay." She did as he'd asked, but didn't look happy about it.

"You know how much I like your mom, right?"

"I guess. It's kinda obvious how you two are always kissin' all the time."

"Yeah, well…" He cleared his throat then grinned. He couldn't stop himself. Connie was the perfect candy that, even after sampling, left him wanting more. "Okay, aside from that, I've known your mom a long time, and with your permission, I'd like to give her this." From the back pocket of his jeans, he withdrew a black velvet box and opened the lid. The one-carat, square-cut sparkler edged in sapphires he'd purchased that morning shone in the sun.

Lindsay gasped. "Is that what I think it is?"

"Technically, it is an engagement ring, but for the moment, with me having to head back to Virginia soon and us still having a lot to talk over, I guess it's more like what back in high school we called a promise ring." Checking the reaction on her sweet face, he was more psyched than he would've expected to find nothing but a cautious smile. He took it as a sign that as crazy as it seemed, he was doing the right thing.

This afternoon, when Connie had jumped to his defense with his mom, he'd asked himself how long had it been since anyone had rescued him?

Granted, in the field, the guys helped one another all the time, but this had been different. Connie had publicly put herself out there for him when airing her personal life wasn't her style.

That, combined with his mother's forgiveness speech, had gotten him thinking. What if this was their second chance at getting things right? Connie hadn't been entirely to blame in their breakup. Obviously something had been lacking in him. A something she'd run off to find in another guy.

But never again. While there were plenty more questions he still needed answers to, for the moment, in his heart of hearts, there was one thing he now craved even more—the promise that this time, their relationship would stick. He wanted to head back to his job with her photo in his chest pocket instead of just in his head. He wanted to fight for her and Lindsay—not just his mom and nameless faces. Bottom line, he wanted it all.

Love. Work. Happiness.

Was it too much to ask?

"Can I try it on?" Lindsay asked, eyes still wide as she studied the ring.

He nodded and she grabbed, shoving it on her pudgy, left hand ring finger, playing with it to better catch the light.

"It's *really* pretty," she said. "Mom's going to be happy."

"Hope so, but at the moment, I'm curious what's going on in your head."

"Can I tell the truth?"

"I wouldn't want anything else," he said, repositioning his cramped legs.

She looked down, played more with the ring. "I'm really excited, but also kinda scared."

"About what?"

"Well…" She gave back the ring. "I like you a whole lot, but someday, if you marry Mom, and then you're my stepdad, does that mean I'll never see my real dad?"

"Heck, no," Garret said, half of him wanting to grab Lindsay up in a hug, the other half wanting to give Nathan a well-aimed right. Garret wanted to be the girl's real father. Rightfully, he should've been. "You can see your dad any time you want. I'll even drive you over."

"Really?" Her expression considerably brightened.

"Sure." Even though having to be civil with Nathan would be Garret's undoing. He'd forgiven Connie, but mostly because he'd villainized his ex-friend. In Garret's mind, Nathan had systematically gone after Connie once Garret decided to join the Navy.

"Cool," Lindsay said. "Okay, well, I guess I have one more question."

"Shoot."

"If you live in Virginia, how're you going to live here? And if you and Mom do someday get married, does that mean we're gonna have to move and stuff, and I'll never get to see any of my friends?"

"Actually," he said, "that's a toughie. One I've been giving a lot of thought to myself." He took a second to think before again speaking. Seeing how good this was going for the moment, he didn't want to blow it. "Since you've been straight with me, I'll do the same for you. I'm not sure what's going to happen with my job. There's a lot to think about. Hopefully, I can get what's called a transfer, but there's not a whole lot of call for what I do around here. I might have to be gone some of the time and then you'd be back in charge of looking after your mom."

She giggled.

"What's so funny?"

"Mom does need looking after sometimes, doesn't she?"

"Hey, give your poor mom a break. We all need looking after, don't you think?"

"I s'pose. So? When're you gonna ask her? And what're you gonna ask? I mean, if you're not really getting engaged, then how come she gets a fancy ring?"

Nipping the inside of his right cheek, he said, "Good question. Wanna help figure it out?"

"WHAT DID YOU DO to my house?" Connie pretty much yelled into the phone the next morning.

Garret held the receiver back a couple inches till she finished her rant about how she didn't have money to finish painting her house right now, and that it wasn't a very funny joke to go around writing graffiti on the front of people's homes, especially when it involved such an important question and couldn't possibly be sincere.

"Whoa," he said. "The whole thing was your daughter's idea. I've already hired painters to come finish the paint job first thing Wednesday morning, and I've never been more sincere about asking any question in my life."

The line went dead silent.

"Connie?"

"I—I think you'd better come over."

Garret grabbed the Caddie keys, then drove like a man possessed to Connie and Lindsay's farm.

By the light of day, his late night project had turned out pretty damned impressive. On the front of the house in neon-pink spray paint, he'd scrawled I Love You then signed his name before tying the ring to a shutter using a pink ribbon Lindsay loaned him. What about his straightforward message had she not understood?

"I'm here!" Garret called out from the back door. Upon entering the kitchen, he found Connie seated at the sun-drenched kitchen table, hands hugging a steaming coffee mug. Odd, seeing how she usually drank tea. Was she needing something stronger? Her expression was mostly serene, yet sadness shadowed her eyes. "What's wrong?"

"Nothing," she said with a slight shake of her head. "Lindsay's off to school after giving me a cryptic goodbye kiss and telling me once I talk to you, I'll be happy."

"You believe her?"

She shrugged. "Want coffee?"

"Sure."

"Have a seat. I'll get you a cup."

"I'll get my own," he said, silently shutting the door, hating this odd vibe between them. He'd asked the woman to marry him. Sort of. This wasn't really the reaction he'd been hoping for. But then what had he expected? In his mind, he was sick of fighting, but he had yet to give her the memo.

"We, um, should probably talk," she said. She set the mug on the table with a clump, sloshing some of the liquid onto her hand. She raised it to her lips. Garret wanted to soothe the pain for her, but how could he begin to do that until she emotionally let him in?

Still standing, washing his face with his hands, Garret said, "Just tell me how you feel, Connie. It's not that I don't want to marry you someday. Just that we're not quite ready—at least I'm not."

"Then why go to all this trouble?"

He took a moment to think. "Truth? I want it made clear to every guy within a hundred miles—especially Nathan—that you're taken."

"But not really? It'd be more like a going-steady kind of thing?"

"Exactly."

"Then, what's with the hefty ring? Last I heard, jewelry wasn't a prerequisite for two people agreeing to date exclusively."

"No," he admitted, "but last time I checked, a ring was the perfect gift for the woman you love. Sorry you apparently disagree. I'll be on my way."

Chapter Twelve

He'd made it to the Caddie when there was a commotion behind him. Hands braced on the vehicle's trunk, he turned to find Connie, running his way, her open white robe flying behind her like low-riding angel's wings. "Stop!"

He shook his head. Sighed. "I'm not doing this, Connie."

"No," she said, pausing to catch her breath. "Just listen. W-when I walked Lindsay to the bus stop this morning, on the return trip I saw your note—and the ring. Lindsay and other kids were shouting out the bus window, and—" Out of breath, she put her hands on her chest. "I couldn't think. It—it all seemed surreal. For as long as I can remember, one by one, I've steadily let go of my dreams. But my dream of some way, somehow marrying you—" She bowed her head and laughed. "That one was a doozy to let go. I thought

I had, but then you came back, turned my whole life upside down. Then you kissed me, and all I could think was maybe the dream wasn't dead after all."

"Connie…" Leaning against the trunk, Garret gazed off to the two-story barn that needed just as much work as the house. "I'll see you this afternoon and call my painter buddy and tell him to step it up. Hopefully he'll get a crew over here today."

"But…"

"I already told you, Connie, I'm tired of talking. Either we make this thing work or we don't. Obviously, we don't, so let's make a clean break while—"

Fiercely shaking her head, easing his ring onto her finger, she said, "I love you. I've always loved you. Please don't go."

Right. Aside from her apparently forgotten dalliance with his best friend?

Standing there, arms crossed, Garret wasn't sure what to think. Thirty seconds earlier, he'd never wanted to see her again. And now…

She stood there, wearing his ring, just like he'd always imagined on countless dark nights. Swimming miles in inky foreign oceans on countless suicide missions, it'd been her, always her, he'd been swimming to. But could he go to her now? After all they'd been through, after all she'd put him through, did he have the energy to take those few more steps that would forever bind him to her?

"If you don't believe me—that I'll be faithful—I can prove it."

Shaking his head, fighting past the wall in his throat, he asked, "What?"

Leaning against the car, covering her face with her hands, she said, "For a decade, I've put off telling you this because of fear. Fear of your reaction. Reprisal. My own past. I don't know why, just that—"

"Put off telling me what?" he asked, eyes narrowed, not sure he wanted to know.

Her eyes shone with a confidence he'd never before seen. "Ever heard that old expression, the truth shall set you free?"

"Sure."

Shaking her head, laughing, she said, "All this time, Nathan was right. He must've told me a hundred times to come clean with you. Tell you what really happened between us, but—"

"What?" Head spinning, leg throbbing, Garret eased himself onto the car's trunk.

"Don't you see? The only proof I've ever needed to show you how much I love you was all the time staring me—us—in the face. I now see this is fate's gentle nudge. Garret, in the little under a year Nathan and I were married, I never slept with him. Aside from a few friendly pecks, I've never even kissed Nathan. It's you I love. Have always loved. Which is why, when I found out I was pregnant—with *your* child—I couldn't bear to tell you because I knew you loved me and that if you stayed here to marry me, then you wouldn't have followed your dreams."

"So you figured why not give up your own dreams?"

"Exactly. I'm so sorry to have kept Lindsay from you all these years. You can't even imagine how sorry. Nathan helped me see that by marrying him, claiming he was Lindsay's father, we'd actually be saving you."

"Saving me?" While a quiet rage grew inside him, Garret sharply laughed.

"Yes. I've always been faithful to you, sweetheart. Not a day has gone by I haven't loved you." Hugging him for all she was worth, she said again, "I'm sorry. Sorry not just for you, but Lindsay."

"Amazing…" He shook his throbbing head. All those nights spent calculating dates. Theorizing about Lindsay being his. Actually wishing she'd been his. Fantasizing about the instant connection he felt with her being real, because he—not Nathan—was her father. After all this time…

On the one hand, he'd just been blessed with an amazing child. On the other, every intimacy he'd shared in the past weeks with Connie had been a lie.

The knowledge of which left him where?

From here, where was he supposed to go?

He sure couldn't return to his old life, knowing he had a kid to raise—even if he'd already missed the first precious ten years of her life. Yet what future did he have in Mule Shoe? Was he supposed to carry on this radio show, sitting two-and-a-half hours each day beside a woman he didn't even want to look at?

How could Connie be so cold? Cruel? What possible explanation could she have for keeping this news from him? Because from where he stood, her pile of excuses of wanting him to follow his dreams didn't hold water.

He'd never before been a crying man, but dammit, today had already been rough and it wasn't nearly over. Eyes stinging, he put his fists over them, asking, "How could you? I trusted you. I was going to marry you."

"I—I love you. I started to tell you so many times, but then one thing led to another and I was seventeen and pregnant and scared. I didn't know what to do. Mom and Dad would've died from shame and then there was you packing up to leave for the Navy, and I—"

"You chose the easy road out."

"You think marrying Nathan over you was easy? Do you think an eighteen-hour labor without you was easy? Trying to make ends meet on my own?"

"But you didn't *have* to do any of that," he said. "That's what I don't get. You and I could've had it all. Seen the world together."

"Sure, Garret, it's easy to paint a rosy picture of what might've been ten years after the fact. Statistically speaking, we probably would've ended up hating each other and divorced within a year. You would've washed out of SEAL training from worry, then resented me and Lindsay the rest of your life."

"That's not true. Stop making me out to be the bad guy."

"There is no bad guy," she said, her voice hoarse from crying. "Yes, what I did was wrong, but at the time, I made what I thought was the best decision. The *only* decision. Would I make the same choice again?" She laughed. "No. But last I heard, they weren't selling life do-overs at Wal-Mart."

He sighed, washed his face with his hands.

"Garret?"

He warily glanced her way. "Yeah?"

"Could I please tell Lindsay? You know, break the news to her gently."

"Sure," he said. "I just—" *I want my daughter's eyes to glow when she talks to me, just like they do when she talks to Nathan.* Chest tight, still reeling from the news himself, Garret nodded. "I'll come by later."

"Thank you."

"I'm only doing good by Lindsay. You're right. My springing this on her isn't smart." *Not if I want to have the kind of relationship she has with Nathan.* Why was his name always popping up? Why couldn't Garret exorcise the man—or, for that matter, Connie—from his life?

"Gotta ask you something," he said.

"Okay."

"If I hadn't called the show, and you'd never known I'd come back to Mule Shoe, would you have ever told me Lindsay's mine?"

"Of course."

"When? Next Christmas? Her sixteenth birthday? High school graduation?"

"Soon. I would've told you soon."

He laughed.

"Haven't you ever had something you loved so much you were terrified of, even for a second, sharing it or letting it go?"

"Haven't you ever heard the saying that if you truly love something, set it free? If it comes back to you, it's yours forever. If not, it was never truly yours in the first place?"

"Garret, we're talking about a child. *My* daughter."

"*Our* daughter."

"Okay, then—" she raised her chin "—I set you free, yet you came back to me. How's your logic working now?"

By god, she was right. But then in his mind, had he ever truly been free of his love for her?

He glanced up to find Connie heading inside. "What are you doing?"

"Wait. I'll be right back."

Upon her return, she handed him a business card. "While I'm talking with Lindsay, it might be a good idea for you to meet with Nathan. He's usually at his dealership till six. The address is on the card."

"I don't want to talk to Nathan." *I don't want to see him—ever be near him—again.*

"It might be good for you to clear the air. Plus, he deserves to know our secret's out. For years, he's wanted me to tell you. I just…couldn't."

"And I can't, for the life of me, understand why."

"I'm sorry for that, too. I'm sorry for everything, Garret, but I know that isn't enough. If I could give you back the time you lost with Lindsay—time I essentially stole from you—I would." She paused. "Are you going to hate me forever?"

Yep. "Forever's a good long while. But for the time being, I can't fathom finding a way to forgive you."

Chapter Thirteen

"Mom?" Lindsay asked after hanging up the phone. From the second she'd gotten home, she'd been all smiles. As soon as she'd come through the back door, she'd charged inside, tossed down her backpack, then grabbed for the phone. She'd been chatting with Emily about bunnies and boys and Barbie dolls ever since.

Constance stood at the kitchen counter, looking up from the cup of minty-smelling tea she'd been stirring for what felt like the last twenty minutes. When she told Lindsay the news, would she hate her? Could Constance really blame her if she did? "Did you have a good talk?"

"Uh-huh. Em's going to have an awesome birthday party. Her mom's gonna get—hey, where's your ring? I thought Garret was askin' you to maybe marry him today?"

"He was. Did."

"Well? Are we getting married? He's cool. A lot of my friends don't like their stepdads, but if you and Garret do get married, I think I'm going to like him a lot."

Was it possible for a heart to break physically, and yet for her still to be standing? Forcing back fresh tears, Constance said, "Sweetie, while you were at school, Garret and I decided not to get married. But—"

"But yesterday afternoon he said he loves you."

"I know, sweetie. Sometimes when grown-ups argue, they don't tell children."

"Yeah, but you always told me I'm your best friend. That means you tell me everything."

"I know, but in this case—"

"So I don't get to see him anymore? What'd you say to him? What'd you do?" Bottom lip trembling, eyes pooling, Lindsay's devastated expression shredded what little remained of Constance's soul.

"Oh, sweetie," she said, crushing her daughter to her. "I'm so sorry. I've already apologized to Garret, but it wasn't enough."

"What'd you do, Mommy?" Lindsay hadn't called her *Mommy* in years, an indicator of just how upset she truly was.

With every fiber of her being, Constance didn't want to tell Lindsay the truth. Maybe it would've been better for her and Garret to tell her together? That she was *their* daughter. But then could there ever be a right way to explain something like this?

"Please, Mom, just tell me the truth."

"Lindsay…" Constance took a deep breath, willed her pounding heart to slow. "Did you notice anything funny about the way you and Garret seemed to get along so well?"

"I don't know. I mean, he seemed really nice and I already love him lots, but I didn't think he was, like, weird or anything."

"I didn't mean like that," Constance said, cupping her hand to her daughter's chin. "I mean, did you find it funny how fast you started to like him?"

"I guess." She wrinkled her nose. "He just seemed really nice."

"Come here," Constance said, taking her daughter's hand to lead her into the living room. "I've got something to show you." Sitting at the rolltop desk, Constance took a key from the chain she always wore around her throat as a reminder to never take her parenting job lightly, and slipped it into a secret compartment her grandfather had shown her years ago.

"Wow! How long have you known about that?"

"A while," Constance said. Trying to stay calm, she withdrew a tissue-wrapped square of ivory cardstock.

"What's that?"

"Your birth certificate."

"But I thought it was in my baby book?"

"It was, but this," she said, setting it on the desk so as not to let her shaking hands alert her daughter to just how upsetting this moment was, "this is your real one."

"My *real* one?" She wrinkled her nose. "What do you mean?"

"Look," Constance said. "Read what it says."

Lindsay picked up the paper, furrowed her brows while silently reading, but moving her lips with each word. "But, Mom, this says… Is this true?"

Tears streaming down her cheeks, Constance nodded.

"I hate you!" Lindsay screamed. "Why did you lie to me my whole life? What's wrong with you?"

While her daughter ran out of the living room and out the back door, Constance sat hugging herself, rocking in her chair. Would this pain ever stop?

She knew this day would come eventually, and now that the truth was out, she realized she was tired of being afraid all the time. Always wishing she could rewrite the past. Dreading the future for fear of Garret or Lindsay uncovering the past. Well, for better or worse, their secret was out. Maybe her daughter and Garret wouldn't ever forgive her, but Constance couldn't go on one more day living with the burden of not being able to forgive herself.

She was bone-deep sorry for what she'd done. There would be no argument from her that in keeping Lindsay's true paternity a secret, she'd committed a horrific act against not just her daughter, but the man she'd claimed to love. But now that they knew the truth, she had to get on with her life.

Tomorrow would be another day. Another chance to make things right. Now all she had to do was find a way to breathe, knowing all hope of Garret ever being back in her life was gone.

"Seeing you is unexpected," Nathan said, strolling through his office door. Garret noted that this time, he didn't bother with the pretense of offering his hand to shake.

"We need to talk."

"We've needed to talk—for the past ten years." He ushered Garret into a plush, oak-paneled office, then shut the door on the bustling auto showroom. Thick red carpet swallowed their footfalls.

Garret had a seat in one of a pair of red leather wing chairs fronting his old pal's massive oak desk. On the wall behind the desk were over a dozen sales awards and photos of Nathan smiling with Oklahoma governors, beauty queens and country music stars.

"Did you love her?" Garret asked.

"Connie?"

Inching to the front of his chair, Garret planted his elbows on Nathan's desk. "It's just us, man. I know about Lindsay. Connie told me this morning."

"Good. It's high time you knew. She's a great kid."

"No one's disputing that. So, tell me. Was this hoax you perpetrated solely altruistic? Or did you want her for yourself?"

Sighing, Nathan leaned back in his chair, momentarily closed his eyes. "Back in high school—shoot, to this day—she wore this perfume. Smelled like the beach. Not sand and sweat, but tropical flowers. Pineapple and a hint of coconut. I wanted her so bad it hurt. Trouble was, she was yours. Always. As your friend, I'm not going to say I liked that fact, but I understood. If she hadn't come to me, confused as hell over what to do about the baby. I swear on my life—Lindsay's life—I never would've made a move."

"Go on…" Garret ignored the muscle ticking in his jaw.

"But she did come to me. And the day she found out she was pregnant, you were blathering about leaving. Showing all your shiny new Navy brochures to anyone who'd stop long enough to see. The decision to keep Lindsay from you started out—for both of us—as an altruistic thing. Think back, Garret, to how psyched you were about leaving. Think how that must've made Connie feel."

"She told me she was happy for me. Then I find out she's sleeping with you?"

"I wish," Nathan said with a sharp laugh. "Nothing *ever* happened between us. Couple times I tried, but there was nothing there. She always saved the best of herself for you."

Now Garret smirked. "She sure had a funny way of showing it."

Straightening papers on his desk, Nathan shrugged. "I'm not going to lie about wanting her for myself. I did everything in my power to make her happy. Showered her with love and gifts. The one thing I never could give her was you."

THE RETURN TRIP to Connie's took an eternity, yet that still wasn't enough time to get his head straight. Winding on a state highway through pasture and stubby oak and maple forests dotted with pine and cedar, Garret tried wrapping his mind around something other than Connie, but nothing worked.

He was due back on the job in a couple weeks. With only a few physical therapy sessions binding him to this place, he should cancel, then finish up on base. Just get out from under this depressing shroud cast over his life.

But then was getting to know Lindsay depressing? No way. She was a miracle. Just that morning, he'd viewed his renewed relationship with Connie as miraculous, too. But now he felt as if the world was crumbling around him.

Approaching Connie's home, one thing became clear. Before he returned to Virginia, he'd see to it that this old place returned to its former glory. He'd make sure to give Lindsay everything she needed.

He parked at the back door, surprised to see Lindsay sitting on the porch steps, brushing her Barbie doll's hair.

"Hey," he said above the crunch of his combat boots chewing gravel.

"Hey." She didn't look up.

"Mind if I join you?"

She shrugged.

He sat, then reached into her plastic doll box to pull out a wild-haired brunette with only one blue eye. "This one looks like she needs a trip to your beauty shop."

"Yeah. I'll do her next."

"I'll get her started," he said, tugging a mini, pink plastic brush out from a tangle of mini clothes. All of this stuff was so small, and these were big kid toys. What must Lindsay's baby stuff have been like? He'd give anything in the world to know.

"It true you're my real dad?"

"Yep." Taking his cue from her, he kept right on brushing, although, considering the wad of hair his doll had, he figured she might be better off going G.I. Jane with a buzz cut. "And I've gotta tell you, from the second your mom told me the news, I was seriously happy."

"Really?" She stopped grooming her doll.

"Oh, heck yeah. Knowing you're mine was better than eating a whole ice-cream store."

"Wow. And you really like ice cream."

"No kidding," he said with a chuckle.

"If you're happy about me, how come you and Mom aren't going to maybe get married? You mad at her? I am. I thought we were best friends, but best friends don't keep secrets like that."

After a sharp exhale, he joked, "I thought you were only s'pose to talk about fun stuff at the beauty parlor?"

Setting her doll in her lap, she fixed him with a sage look well beyond her years. "This isn't a beauty shop, but the back porch."

"Oh. Well, in that case…" He cleared his throat.

"Don't you love Mom anymore? I'm thinking maybe I don't."

"Sure you do. It's not that simple," he said. "She's your mom. Understandably you're upset with her now, but in time, while you may not like or understand what she did, you'll learn to deal with it." Great advice. Too bad there wasn't a snowball's chance in hell of him following it. Grinning, he nudged Lindsay's shoulder.

"What about Dad—Nathan?"

"What about him?" Garret asked, preferring to avoid the subject altogether.

"If you're my real dad, what's he?"

As much as it pains me to say it, "He's always going to be a father to you, kiddo. He loves you, too. Now you'll just have two dads." Surprisingly the knowledge didn't cut quite as deeply as Garret had feared. His talk with Nathan had stolen a lot of his fury's flame. Man to man, Nathan had told him the truth, and Garret did now believe that, at the time, his two friends had thought they'd been doing him a favor. He'd also been oddly happy to learn even Nathan's comfortable lifestyle hadn't been enough to lure Connie away.

"That's what Mom said."

"So," Garret said after a deep breath. "Did she also tell you that tonight we're going to have dinner with my mom—your grandma?"

"Yeah. I'm kind of nervous about that. My grandma Victoria—she's my other dad's mom—lives in West Palm Beach. Whenever I see her, she likes me to be real clean. Is your mom like that?"

"She'll make you wash your hands before dinner, but other than that, I think you're good to go."

"Okay."

The screen door creaked open and Connie poked her head outside. Just the sight of her still made him crazy with wanting, but *wanting* was no longer good enough. He also had to trust her. And learning she was capable of a deception this great had rocked him to his core. When he one day married, he wanted a woman with no secrets. No dark corners to which she retreated. If she had a problem, she'd turn to him for help—not his best friend.

"Hey, guys," she said. "You two ready to go?"

Careful not to look anywhere near her mother, Lindsay nodded. "Let me put my dolls away. You done with her?" she asked Garret, nodding toward his frizzy-haired brunette.

"Yeah," he said, feeling as if the moment had taken on added significance. "I'm done with her."

LONG AFTER LINDSAY and Connie had left, Garret stood at the kitchen sink, washing dishes while his mother dried. "You and Lindsay seemed to get along well," he said.

"She's an angel. I still can't believe she's part of our family."

They did the chore awhile in companionable silence, before Audrey looked at her son. "I know you're still very upset about this and it's completely understandable, but I believe Constance was sincere about having wanted you to follow your dreams and, you have to admit, you've led a pretty full life. Traveling the world, carrying out your covert missions. Honestly, deep in your heart, can you tell me you'd have been happier here? Getting married and settling down straight out of high school?"

He clenched his jaw, wishing she'd stay out of his business.

If he had a crystal ball, he'd know whether or not leading a more traditional life would've been better. But how was he supposed to know? Connie had never given him the choice.

"Give it time," his mother continued. "You've been through an awful lot these past few months. Let it all sink in. Maybe a few more months— even years—down the road, you'll be able to forgive Connie."

Rolling his eyes, he said, "Listen to you, rattling on like some relationship expert. When I head back to Virginia, how about you take my place on Connie's show and answer some calls?"

"Watch it, Mr. Smarty Pants," she said with a grin. "Speaking of callers, your CO phoned. He'd like you to contact him right away. Said it didn't matter what time."

"Why didn't you tell me sooner?" he asked, drying the last dish and heading to the kitchen phone.

"Sorry, but with everything that's happened I forgot."

He snorted, Forgetfulness seemed to be catching among the women in his life. Good thing for him his mom hadn't failed to remember quite as big a doozy as Connie.

Chapter Fourteen

A few hours later, Garret found himself seated on an uncomfortable nylon cargo seat in the belly of a C-130, the engine noise so loud he couldn't have heard his own voice. With the memory of Connie's sweet, simple scent masked by jet fuel, he didn't think his mood could get much darker.

Then it occurred to him that because he'd been so abruptly called back to active duty, he hadn't even given Lindsay a proper goodbye.

Seeing how by noon tomorrow, he'd be over the Atlantic, he'd try giving his daughter a ring before meeting up with his team in Virginia.

His daughter.

The phrase still had a nice sound. Would've been even nicer had he had the chance to hold her when she'd been a baby. He knew full well in his heart that had Connie told him she was pregnant, he would've done right by her and Lindsay. He would've married her and taken her with him. Yes, times would've been tough, but at least they would've been together. What about that had Connie failed to see? What had ever made her think he wouldn't have been supportive or sympathetic toward her situation—*their* situation? Hell, it wasn't as if he hadn't been partly responsible for the trouble she'd found herself in.

The sun was just peaking over the horizon by the time the pilots landed at his base. He thanked the flight crew, then hitched a ride on a supply truck to his headquarters.

Once there, he bribed the yeoman manning the desk to borrow his cell—Garret's was dead—then headed outside into tentative morning sun. He found a concrete picnic table on a weary patch of grass and had a seat.

A flock of sparrows tittered over what looked like the remains of someone's Pop-Tarts.

He was running out of time to put in a call he knew was too early for Lindsay to even be awake enough to comprehend. But then, seeing how he didn't know when he'd get a chance to call again, it wasn't as if he had much choice.

The phone rang five times before being picked up.

"Hello?" Connie said, her voice hoarse.

"Connie," he said, trying not to picture her standing in the sun-flooded kitchen, looking sleepy-sexy with her dark hair a tousled mess. "I need to talk to Lindsay."

"She's sleeping. Can you call back later?"

He sighed. "I'll be in some godforsaken third world country tomorrow, otherwise I wouldn't be calling this early."

"W-where are you?"

"Back on base. My CO called. I flew out last night."

"That eager to get away from me?"

"My leaving has nothing to do with you. Don't flatter yourself."

"Do you have to be so cold? How many times do I have to apologize? Is there ever going to be a day when you don't hate me? Garret, I'm sorry. You have no idea of how sorry I am, and if you'd just let me—"

"Yo, Underwood! You ready to kick some terrorist ass?"

His pal, Brick Marchetti, a big, strapping Kansas boy, jogged to Garret's formerly private spot. "The old man says he's starting the briefing in ten."

Covering the phone's mouthpiece, Garret said, "Be right there." To Connie, he said, "Right now, I need you to get my daughter on the phone."

"O-okay."

He heard her walking through the kitchen to the stairs, going up until she reached the ninth step that had that squeak he'd been meaning to fix. Eyes closed, he saw every minute sashay of her hips. The soft curve of her luscious backside. He wanted her with biting, exquisite hardness, which was wrong, considering how he would barely be in the same room with her right now.

"Hello?" said his sleepy little girl.

"Hey, squirt," he said past the lump in his throat.

"Garret?"

"Yeah, it's me."

"Why're you callin' so early? And aren't you coming over today to help clean my rabbit house?"

Closing his eyes and praying for the right words, Garret said, "I'm sorry, squirt, but my boss called, and I have to go out of town for a while."

"How long?"

"I don't know."

"But what about my school play? I thought you were staying here for a while?"

"I was, but—" He'd been on the verge of saying he was really busy, but he needed her to understand his job was more than that. That he wouldn't dream of leaving her or missing her performance if it wasn't a matter of life and death. So what did he say when he wanted to hang with her this after-noon with every fiber of his being, but it wasn't possible? "Look, angel, I'm going to be straight with you. Remember how I told you sometimes my job would take me away from you and your mom?"

"Yeah."

"Well, I got a call last night from my boss and this is one of those times. I hate leaving you now, you know, when we were getting to be good friends, but I want you to know I will be back. I'll—"

"Underwood! CO says you gotta come—*now!*"

Squeezing his eyes shut, willing them to stop stinging, Garret said, "Linds, honey, I've got to go, but please know I love you."

"I know," she said with a sniffle. "I love you, too…Dad."

Dad. Had any word ever sounded sweeter?

Even though it was tough speaking, he said, "When I get home, we'll go for ice cream and to the Tulsa Zoo and even back to the mall to get some great stuff for your room." Home. There was another great word. While he didn't have a clue as to how he'd work out the logistics, he knew Mule Shoe would one day again be his home. He wanted to share as much time as possible with his little girl while she was still little.

And her mother? You also want to spend time with her? He scowled.

Lindsay asked, "Can we get more decorations for the rabbit house?"

"Sure." *Anything to see a smile in your eyes.*

"What about Mom? Can she come?"

"Underwood! If you're not in the CO's office in one minute, he says he's court-martialing you!"

"Squirt, I'm in big trouble here, but—"

"I know," she said, suddenly sounding way more grown-up than ten. "I heard."

For the first time since joining the Navy, he wished he was headed off to a nine-to-five desk job.

"Be careful, okay?"

"I will, honey. You, too."

Garret closed the flip phone, not just ending the call, but a chapter of his life. Thanks to Connie, it'd been a long time coming, but finally, finally, he was a real father.

"DECK!" GARRET SHOUTED to the rest of his team immersed in an inky ocean-black night, ducking just before the sniper on the Athens-based research ship *nOLitzh* fired off his next rounds. Adrenaline pumping, dressed in black and camouflage tactical gear, MP5 in hand, Garret cursed this godforsaken stretch of water called the Gulf of Aden, where the U.S. State Department had received a cry for help from a group of American students and their teachers who'd been taken hostage by an extremist terrorist group.

Garret crawled on his belly, taking shelter

behind a rigid inflatable. Humidity had to be a hundred and twenty percent, which made for a fun ride on a wind-driven sea sporting seven-foot swells. A can of WD-40 rolled across the steel deck, making a hellacious clatter. Garret grabbed for it, securing it beneath the inflatable.

Left leg aching from exertion he apparently wasn't quite ready for, he scrambled left, firing his own rounds.

Judging by the death cry he heard up near the bow, the sniper was history.

Waving to his team, Garret leaped to his feet, dodging left, then right toward the metal stairs leading to the ship's main deck—the spot rumored to be the holding place for the U.S. passengers.

After taking out three more snipers, he and his team fanned with defensive postures around the steel, primary entrance door.

Getting to this point had been too easy, meaning his internal alarm pealed at full tilt. What was he missing? Booby traps? Considering what each family would be willing to pay to get their loved ones back, unless the bad guys were dumb, they weren't going to surrender easy.

Struggling to get his head back into commando mode after having lived the past weeks dodging Connie's emotional bullets, Garret squinted through his night vision goggles around the cabin's edge. At this level, the only exterior deck was aft, meaning the terrorists would presumably have to go out and over or out and under to get to where Garret was waiting.

Crouching and darting, he paused three feet from the door, scanning for signs of a trap. "Got ya," he said under his breath upon finding a thread-thin trip wire. He traced it back to its source—enough cheap explosives to blow this ship and its occupants straight to hell.

Using hand signals each man in turn passed down the line, he called for his bomb expert, while the rest of the team held tight till receiving an all clear.

From there came the part of these gigs Garret liked best—getting the prize.

He'd just motioned for the remainder of his guys not on perimeter guard duty to come around to his position when the cabin's steel door burst open and a swarming cloud of machine-gun-toting extremists buzzed through.

"Fall back!" Garret shouted. "Take cover!"

After a twenty-minute shoot-out resulted in three, gut-wrenching casualties for the good guys—including Marchetti—and total annihilation for the bad, Garret led the team inside to release the hostages.

Through the endless day and night it took to get the hostages checked out healthwise, then get them safely to a U.S. base in Germany, Garret held tight to his numbness.

Not until he saw a few of the family members who'd flown over the pond to meet up with their loved ones did it occur to him that along with Marchetti and the other's, he also could've died.

Before learning of Lindsay, Garret had sported an untouchable cloak of invincibility. But now… having already lost Connie and having just now found his daughter, for first time ever, he was consumed by his mortality's weight.

Life wasn't a video game played out on foreign oceans while breathing in salty air. It was waking up to share mugs of coffee with the woman you loved. Going to cheer on your daughter in her school play. Eating tons of ice cream and his mom's chocolate chip cookies.

In a split second, Garret chose to forgive Connie by letting go his fury over having been duped for the past ten years. After today, seeing those families reunited, it didn't matter why he and Connie had been apart, just that they spent every day of the rest of whatever remained of their lives together.

Finding a phone, he dialed her number, not caring what time it was back in Oklahoma, just needing to let them know he was safe and coming home.

"RENEE-MARIE? Do you have my next caller?" Though it'd only been a week since her last show with Garret, Constance was as bored with herself as listeners seemed to be. Just as Garret had brought her spirit to life, he'd also breathed life into the show. She was tweaking the format to try to add more general-interest topics, but the transition was slow going.

And truthfully, she got the impression Felix was only keeping her on air in hopes that Garret made good on his promise to call in occasionally.

"Sure do," the producer said. "Callie on line one has a question about what to wear to her cousin's baby shower."

"Welcome, Callie. How may I be of assistance?"

"First, I just wanna say how much I miss Military Man, and I'm really sad about things between you two not working out."

"Thank you." Constance cupped her throbbing forehead. Would her life ever be Garret-free? *Do you really want it to be?* That was hardly the issue, seeing how she hadn't had all that much choice in his leaving. "And your question?"

"Oh, yes. Well, I was wondering if it's inappropriate to wear red to a baby shower?"

The question she once would've put such thought into answering now struck her as ludicrous. Her beautiful family had fallen apart and she didn't care about baby shower apparel or thank-you notes or napkin folds. Still, the show must go on and all that, so she took a deep breath and said, "Yes. It's highly inappropriate to wear red to a baby shower." Click. She disconnected the caller. "Renee-Marie, who's my next victim?"

"Um, how about Reggie on line four."

"Welcome, Reggie. How may I be of service?"

"Y'all aren't going to bite my head off like you did Callie, are you?" The man's thick Southern drawl reverberated through her, reminding her in subtle ways of Garret. Great. Because she really needed one more thing to remind her how much she missed him.

"No, sir, I promise not to let my cranky mood affect you. And, Callie, if you're still out there, sorry to be so snippy. *Do* wear red or blaze orange or purple. Just go to that shower and have a wonderful time hanging out laughing and eating cake with loved ones, not worrying about what everyone's wearing. Okay, Reggie, how may I be of service?"

"I know this is off topic," he said, his accent thicker than ever, *"but I was wondrin' if you could help me out of one heckuva pickle."*

"I'll certainly try," she said, easing forward in her seat, resting her elbows on the desk.

"You see, it's like this. I broke things off with my girl. Said things I shouldn't have. But now I want her back, only I'm not quite sure of the proper etiquette to go about wooing her back into my favor."

"First of all," Constance said with a faint smile, "I like that word—*wooing*—evokes all sorts of wonderful connotations. Surprise her with goofy little wonders like filling a friend's boathouse with candles." *Candles you stole from your mother's church.* "Or, go for the grand romantic gesture like painting her house."

"That's romantic?"

She laughed. "Trust me. To a woman who badly needs her house painted, it'll flood her with want for you."

"That's it?"

"There's a lot more to it than that. You'll want to go in with an attitude of forgiveness—and trust that whatever the two of you didn't see eye to eye on the first time around, that this time, you'll get things right."

"And if I do all that, and she still won't take me back?"

She laughed. "You sound like a sweet guy, Reggie. If she won't have you, I sure will."

"The hell you will," the caller said, his voice changing to an-all-too-familiar growl. The studio door opened and in walked Garret, cell phone to his ear. He flipped it shut.

Renee-Marie said with a smile, "Sorry, Miss Manners, but we seem to have lost the call."

"Garret…" Constance's heart lurched somewhere between her throat and stomach. "Th-that was you?"

He nodded.

"But…"

"I told you I loved you, Connie. Granted, things haven't exactly worked out as either of us hoped, but if you'll still have me, I'd like to spend the rest of my life making it up to you and our little girl."

Crying, laughing, Constance rose to run to him. But in the cramped booth, her run turned out to be more like a leap straight into his outstretched arms. "I can't believe you're back."

"Where else would I be?"

She didn't care, dousing him in a hundred tiny shimmering kisses. "I love you, I love you, I—"

"God, baby," he said, briefly coming up for breath, hands in her hair, then gliding down her back. "I love you, too."

Finding herself the show's temporary host, Renee-Marie cleared her throat. "In case some of you out there are wondering why we suddenly have dead air, it seems a certain man finally took his head out of his behind long enough to see the angel standing in front of him. Now I'm no expert on manners, but I'd say the kissing goin' on is highly inappropriate for office behavior. But seeing how it's all in the name of love, we'll just leave those two on their own while I run this spot from Big Hal's Tires."

Even though Renee-Marie pressed the button for commercial, Miss Manners and the Military Man's phone lines glowed solid red.

Epilogue

Two Years Later

Constance leaned into the mic, loving the comfort and rich smell of her supple leather chair in the newly refurbished broadcast booth Felix had finally agreed to provide—assuming Miss Manners and the Military Man agreed to signing a new five-year syndication contract. Considering the deal provided enough cash to pay for not only her ongoing college education, but Lindsay's and even the baby who was on the way, she and Garret had had no problem signing.

"For those of you just joining us in Madison, Wisconsin," she said, grinning toward her handsome hubby, "we'd like to thank you for being our three hundredth station to carry the show. It's our sincere hope that we'll be able to both entertain and inform without offending."

Garret cleared his throat. "Excuse me, but my favorite part of this gig is offending."

Constance rolled her eyes. "Feel free to ignore him. He's just cranky because the baby kept him up all night."

"Hey," Garret complained, "how was I supposed to know the kid could kick like that before he even popped out? I mean, all I was doing was trying to spoon with my wife, when from out of nowhere, she flops over and BAM—this kid kicks me in the gut."

"Oh, now please, quit exaggerating. And anyway," she said with a sexy purr, "it would take a lot to faze that six-pack of yours."

"You like my six-pack?" Easing back in his chair, he raised his camo-green T-shirt, baring those abs for only her to see.

Copping a feel of his warm, smooth skin, she closed her eyes and smiled. "Ladies, if you have a hankering for heaven, might I suggest running out to find your own military man?"

In her brand spankin' new production booth, Renee-Marie rolled her eyes and grinned.

* * * * *

Happily ever after is just the beginning...

Turn the page for a sneak preview of
DANCING ON SUNDAY AFTERNOONS
by Linda Cardillo

Harlequin Everlasting—Every great love
has a story to tell.™

A brand-new line from Harlequin Books
launching this February!

Prologue

Giulia D'Orazio
1983

I had two husbands—Paolo and Salvatore.

Salvatore and I were married for thirty-two years. I still live in the house he bought for us; I still sleep in our bed. All around me are the signs of our life together. My bedroom window looks out over the garden he planted. In the middle of the city, he coaxed tomatoes, peppers, zucchini—even grapes for his wine—out of the ground. On weekends, he used to drive up to his cousin's farm in Waterbury and bring back manure. In the winter, he wrapped the peach tree and the fig tree with rags and black rubber hoses against the cold, his massive, coarse hands gentling those trees as if they were his fragile-skinned babies. My neighbor, Dominic Grazza, does that for me now. My boys have no time for the garden.

In the front of the house, Salvatore planted roses. The roses I take care of myself. They are giant, cream-colored, fragrant. In the afternoons, I like to sit out on the porch with my coffee, protected from the eyes of the neighborhood by that curtain of flowers.

Salvatore died in this house thirty-five years ago. In the last months, he lay on the sofa in the parlor so he could be in the middle of everything. Except for the two oldest boys, all the children were still at home and we ate together every evening. Salvatore could see the dining room table from the sofa, and he could hear everything that was said. "I'm not dead, yet," he told me. "I want to know what's going on."

When my first grandchild, Cara, was born, we brought her to him, and he held her on his chest, stroking her tiny head. Sometimes they fell asleep together.

Over on the radiator cover in the corner of the parlor is the portrait Salvatore and I had taken on our twenty-fifth anniversary. This brooch I'm wearing today, with the diamonds—I'm wearing it in the photograph also—Salvatore gave it to me that day. Upstairs on my dresser is a jewelry box filled with necklaces and bracelets and earrings. All from Salvatore.

I am surrounded by the things Salvatore gave me, or did for me. But, God forgive me, as I lie alone now in my bed, it is Paolo I remember.

Paolo left me nothing. Nothing, that is, that my family, especially my sisters, thought had any value. No house. No diamonds. Not even a photograph.

But after he was gone, and I could catch my breath from the pain, I knew that I still had something. In the middle of the night, I sat alone and held them in my hands, reading the words over and over until I heard his voice in my head. I had Paolo's letters.

This February…

HARLEQUIN® *Romance*®

What a month!

In February watch for

Rancher and Protector
Part of the Western Weddings miniseries
BY JUDY CHRISTENBERRY

The Boss's Pregnancy Proposal
BY RAYE MORGAN

Also in February, expect
MORE of what you love
as the Harlequin Romance line
increases to six titles per month.

REQUEST YOUR FREE BOOKS!
2 FREE NOVELS PLUS 2
FREE GIFTS!

American ROMANCE®

Heart, Home & Happiness!

YES! Please send me 2 FREE Harlequin American Romance® novels and my 2 FREE gifts. After receiving them, if I don't wish to receive any more books, I can return the shipping statement marked "cancel." If I don't cancel, I will receive 4 brand-new novels every month and be billed just $4.24 per book in the U.S., or $4.99 per book in Canada, plus 25¢ shipping and handling per book and applicable taxes, if any*. That's a savings of close to 15% off the cover price! I understand that accepting the 2 free books and gifts places me under no obligation to buy anything. I can always return a shipment and cancel at any time. Even if I never buy another book from Harlequin, the two free books and gifts are mine to keep forever.

154 HDN EEZK   354 HDN EEZV

Name _____ (PLEASE PRINT)

Address _____ Apt. #

City _____ State/Prov. _____ Zip/Postal Code

Signature (if under 18, a parent or guardian must sign)

Mail to the **Harlequin Reader Service®**:
IN U.S.A.: P.O. Box 1867, Buffalo, NY 14240-1867
IN CANADA: P.O. Box 609, Fort Erie, Ontario L2A 5X3

Not valid to current Harlequin American Romance subscribers.

Want to try two free books from another line?
Call 1-800-873-8635 or visit www.morefreebooks.com.

* Terms and prices subject to change without notice. NY residents add applicable sales tax. Canadian residents will be charged applicable provincial taxes and GST. This offer is limited to one order per household. All orders subject to approval. Credit or debit balances in a customer's account(s) may be offset by any other outstanding balance owed by or to the customer. Please allow 4 to 6 weeks for delivery.

Your Privacy: Harlequin is committed to protecting your privacy. Our Privacy Policy is available online at www.eHarlequin.com or upon request from the Reader Service. From time to time we make our lists of customers available to reputable firms who may have a product or service of interest to you. If you would prefer we not share your name and address, please check here. ☐

HAR07

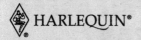

HARLEQUIN®

American ROMANCE®

COMING NEXT MONTH

#1149 THE DOCTOR'S LITTLE SECRET by Jacqueline Diamond
Fatherhood
Dr. Russ McKenzie doesn't have much in common with shoot-from-the-hip
policewoman Rachel Byers. Nevertheless, he shares his little secret with her.
Soon the two of them could be keeping it for life!

#1150 HER PERFECT HERO by Kara Lennox
Firehouse 59
The firefighters of Firehouse 59 are stunned when Julie Polk decides to convert
a local hangout into a *tearoom!* Determined not to let that happen, they elect
resident Casanova Tony Veracruz to sweet-talk the blonde into changing her mind.
But when Tony wants more than just a fling with Julie, he's not sure where his
loyalties lie....

#1151 ONCE A COWBOY by Linda Warren
Brodie Hayes is a former rodeo star, now a rancher—a cowboy through and
through. Yet when he finds out some shocking news about the circumstances
of his birth, he begins to question his identity. Luckily, private investigator
Alexandra Donovan is there to help him find the truth—but will it really
change who he is?

#1152 THE SHERIFF'S SECOND CHANCE by Leandra Logan
When Ethan Taggert, sheriff of Maple Junction, Wisconsin, hears
Kelsey Graham is coming home for the first time in ten years, he wants to
be there when she arrives. Not only is he eagerly anticipating seeing his former
crush, he's also there to protect her. After all, there's a reason she couldn't
return home before now....

www.eHarlequin.com

HARCNM0107